THE L.

SERIES TITLES

The Waterman
Gary Schanbacher

Close Call
Kim Suhr

Signs of the Imminent Apocalypse and Other Stories
Heidi Bell

What We Might Become
Sara Reish Desmond

The Silver State Stories
Michael Darcher

An Instinct for Movement
Michael Mattes

The Machine We Trust
Tim Conrad

Gridlock
Brett Biebel

Salt Folk
Ryan Habermeyer

The Commission of Inquiry
Patrick Nevins

Maximum Speed
Kevin Clouther

Reach Her in This Light
Jane Curtis

The Spirit in My Shoes
John Michael Cummings

The Effects of Urban Renewal on Mid-Century America and Other Crime Stories
Jeff Esterholm

What Makes You Think You're Supposed to Feel Better
Jody Hobbs Hesler

Fugitive Daydreams
Leah McCormack

Hoist House: A Novella & Stories
Jenny Robertson

Finding the Bones: Stories & A Novella
Nikki Kallio

Self-Defense
Corey Mertes

Where Are Your People From?
James B. De Monte

Sometimes Creek
Steve Fox

The Plagues
Joe Baumann

The Clayfields
Elise Gregory

Kind of Blue
Christopher Chambers

Evangelina Everyday
Dawn Burns

Township
Jamie Lyn Smith

Responsible Adults
Patricia Ann McNair

Great Escapes from Detroit
Joseph O'Malley

Nothing to Lose
Kim Suhr

The Appointed Hour
Susanne Davis

PRAISE FOR

THE WATERMAN

"In Gary Schanbacher's third book, the novel-in-stories *The Waterman*, he continues his exploration of difficult lives set in gorgeous, sometimes-dangerous landscapes. Here, we follow the full arc of Clayton Royster's life, from the young man fishing on the beach to the old man overhearing his nurse and loved ones plan his final years or days. Schanbacher is a master at distilling quick moments of love, loss, emotion, confusion, all couched in elegant, direct prose. This novel is a moving testament to what fulfillment can mean, what regret can engender, how simple desire can tangle a life."

—WILLIAM HAYWOOD HENDERSON
author of *Augusta Locke*

"*The Waterman* reaffirms my commitment to read everything Gary Schanbacher writes. Set against the seductive and often perilous backdrop of coastal Virginia, this novel-in-stories is both a celebration of fierce independence and an affirmation of the profound power of human connection. This is a gorgeous collection populated with memorable, original characters. Clayton Royster, the waterman of the title, is drawn so vividly that I feel I have known him all my life."

—TIFFANY QUAY TYSON
author of *The Past is Never*

"In *The Waterman*, Gary Schanbacher performs a miraculous feat, riding the fierce wave of naturalism to gracefully land in the sands of community. Clayton's lifelong affair with the sea gives as much as it takes, and readers will leave his story sobered and heartened both."

—JENNIFER WORTMAN
author of *This. This. This. Is. Love. Love. Love.*

"*The Waterman* has a spare, crystalline beauty to it, much like the ocean on a clear day. It's also a story whose characters fascinate when—or perhaps because—they aren't quite as clear on their motivations. One can't help but care about each of them as they embrace the travails of life and place in the only way they know how: by showing, in some small way, their love for one another, an affection they lack the words to express."

—MICHAEL HENRY
author of *Active Gods*

THE
WATERMAN

THE
WATERMAN

STORIES

GARY
SCHANBACHER

CORNERSTONE PRESS
UNIVERSITY OF WISCONSIN-STEVENS POINT

Cornerstone Press, Stevens Point, Wisconsin 54481
Copyright © 2024 Gary Schanbacher
www.uwsp.edu/cornerstone

Printed in the United States of America by
Point Print and Design Studio, Stevens Point, Wisconsin

Library of Congress Control Number: 2024940028
ISBN: 978-1-960329-42-4

Portions of the title story, "The Waterman," first appeared in *Migration Patterns: Stories* (2007). Used by permission of Chicago Review Press.

Cover art: Winslow Homer. "Breaking Storm, Coast of Maine," 1894. The Art Institute of Chicago. This information, which is available on the object page for each work, is also made available under Creative Commons Zero (CC0).

Cornerstone Press titles are produced in courses and internships offered by the Department of English at the University of Wisconsin–Stevens Point.

DIRECTOR & PUBLISHER
Dr. Ross K. Tangedal

EXECUTIVE EDITORS
Jeff Snowbarger, Freesia McKee

EDITORIAL DIRECTOR
Ellie Atkinson

SENIOR EDITORS
Brett Hill, Grace Dahl

PRESS STAFF
Paige Biever, Sam Bjork, Carolyn Czerwinski, Gwen Goetter, Sophie McPherson, Eva Nielsen, Natalie Reiter, Angelina Sherman, Holly White, Ava Willett

For Leslee, who loved the sand and sea.

CONTENTS

The Waterman 1

The Lies We Tell Ourselves 25

Uncle Billy's Bar & Grille 49

The Accident 63

The Last Dune 81

Old Injuries 99

Giddy's Pet & Play 115

Taking Stock 133

Acknowledgments 141

To me the sea is a continual miracle,
The fishes that swim—the rocks—the motion of the waves—the
*   ships with men in them,*
What stranger miracles are there?

—Walt Whitman

THE WATERMAN

Sand Point, June 1955

Clayton Royster eased his boat along the brackish channel that led from the bay to the dock behind the seafood market. The market was located along the one road into Sand Point, Virginia, a small town at the head of a peninsula jutting between the Atlantic Ocean to the east and the broad saltmarsh bay to the west. Clayton tied off to the dock cleats, unloaded two baskets brimming with blue crabs and carried them around front. Walter's Market was a moss-stained, whitewashed cinderblock building with a broad-planked entrance porch and a raw sheet metal roof. The building housed the store in front and living quarters in back. The day was early yet, the "Closed" sign still posted on the door, so he wet down the crabs from the outside spigot and slipped a nickel into the red vending machine on the porch and sat on the step drinking his soda and picking under his fingernails with his pocketknife. The hands, the split nails, cracked knuckles, and calluses fanning across his palms, were the hands of a man older than Clayton's twenty-three years. But, he was proud of them, of what they represented, the seasons crabbing in the bay and fishing in the open sea, more seasons in his few years than most spend in a lifetime. If his hands did not give him away, his deeply tanned face, his brown hair tinted auburn by the elements, the beginning of crow's feet at the corners of his eyes, and his slight but perpetual squint from the sun's glare surely would—he was a waterman.

Soon came a ruckus from inside and Walter's bulk filled the doorway, white T-shirt straining across his gut, dungarees held up by suspenders. He glanced at Clayton and then turned and hollered toward the back room, "Wish I could get them eggs done right just once."

Clayton stood. "Got your crabs here." Walter turned his scowl back on Clayton and then noticed the baskets.

"Let's take a look." He stepped from the door and lifted the burlap bag covering the crabs. As he assessed the catch, Clayton looked past him to Loretta, who had come barefoot onto the porch in a sleeveless shift, her strawberry hair pulled into a ponytail. She crossed her arms at her chest and stared openly at him, her pale eyes full of trials.

Walter straightened and scratched at a patch of belly exposed at his beltline. "I'll be honest with you, son. That is a right scrawny lot. I can go maybe seven-fifty a bushel."

They both knew within a narrow range what price they would settle on, but the haggle was an expected part of doing business.

"You're probably right," Clayton said. "I should dump them back into the bay to grow up."

"I might see my way to eight," Walter said. "Not a penny more." Clayton nodded.

When Walter walked inside to retrieve payment, Clayton stepped toward Loretta. "Can you get free for a bit?"

"Maybe. He's talking about going to Pungo to see about getting sweet corn for the weekend."

Clayton bent to retie his boot and allowed the back of his hand to brush her calf just to feel the electricity rush through him. He rose and backed away at the sound of Walter returning.

Mid-day, Clayton watched from a stand of pin oaks as Walter climbed into his truck and pulled away, raising a plume of white dust from the crushed shell roadbed. Inside the market, he idled beside a shelf displaying an assortment of carvings from local craftsmen—decoys, sand pipers, gulls—and scanned the dry good isles to ensure the store was free of customers. Satisfied, he walked toward the back and found Loretta behind the checkout counter, sipping from a glass of lemonade, a small rotating fan stirring her hair. He embraced her, tasted the tartness on her lips, her tongue, and he ran his hand down the smooth curve of her back, and bent to kiss the welt showing on her arm. "He do this to you?"

She took his hand and pulled him toward the ice room. "Hurry. He won't be gone long."

At First Sight, May 1950

CLAYTON FIRST LAID EYES ON Loretta five years earlier, in May of 1950. He was walking the beach with his fishing gear when from the south wended the black dot of a pickup on the hard pack. The truck eventually pulled close and a man who looked to be Clayton's father's age, but with loose jowls, raised a finger to the bill of his cap as they passed, but did not stop. A black-and-tan hound occupied the passenger seat, its long face hanging from the window. In the bed of the pickup, an aged lady sat in a rocking chair and beside her a girl shared space with two mattresses and a few wooden crates. Clayton noticed the girl immediately, fifteen or sixteen he guessed, and slender as a surf rod. He willed her to glance his way, but she ignored him, looking out to sea instead. Clayton watched the truck until it disappeared between two dunes toward the blacktop that led into town.

People talked about the newcomers. The man, Walter Pine, had purchased the old Henley market, and quickly gained notice for being fawning with customers, contentious with suppliers, and disengaged with most everyone else.

"A bit standoffish," some said of the Pine family, who by and large kept to themselves. "The elderly lady is sickly, I hear."

"His mother?"

"So I'm told. The girl tends to her."

"His daughter?"

"Wife."

"The girl?"

"Loretta Pine. His wife."

"There has to be a tale behind that match."

Indeed, there was. The most repeated version had her daddy involved in some construction accident that left him alive, but feeble-minded. The family needed help getting by, children by the score, and it seemed Walter came up with the solution.

Clayton began selling crabs to Walter during that first summer. He found reasons to hang around the store just to catch sight of Loretta. They began visiting whenever Walter was away, innocently at first, just two young people passing the time. He'd talk of his dream—a commercial boat: a thirty-footer, mahogany hull, Cummings diesel, something that would allow him to earn a living on the water full-time. Loretta told of her family, the pride she took in being able to help provide for them through Walter and the market.

Clayton admired her sense of obligation. He'd left his family at sixteen when his father decided to take an insurance job in Richmond. Clayton declined to move and instead went to work at Sonny Ferrell's ESSO station after school and lived in a spare room that Sonny and his wife were never able to fill with a child of their own.

When Walter's mother died at the beginning of their second summer season in Sand Point, Walter reluctantly left Loretta in charge of the store while he carted his mother back south for burial. During his absence, one thing led to another between Loretta and Clayton.

Even during an interminable two-year stint drafted into the Army, Clayton ferried back to Sand Point on every furlough from Fort Eustis, and he and Loretta continued to sneak into the ice room for quick, urgent couplings, and snatches of conversation. But that was the whole of it. Once returned and back on the water, Clayton worried about his life spinning in circles, impatient to get on with things but unable to let go of Loretta, and she unwilling to let go of Walter's money. They'd nearly been caught a half-dozen times but always their luck held.

Sand Point, ice room, June 1955

UNTIL IT DIDN'T.

From the ice room, a sound out front startled them. Clayton tucked to a corner as Loretta ladled a bucket of ice chips and carried it to the display counter. Clayton caught sight of Walter leaning against the counter, red-faced, heaving like a bellows.

"Mr. Pine," Loretta said. "I thought you were headed to Pungo."

"Goddamned truck quit on me a mile out. Had to walk back in this goddamned heat."

"Let me get you some water."

"Goddamned Zed Phelps passed me right by and didn't slow a tick. I'll remember that son-of-a-bitch."

"Maybe some lemonade?"

"Bring me a beer."

"I don't think there is any beer."

"There's beer. Find it."

"I can't find what's not there."

"Watch that mouth." Walter jabbed a finger towards Loretta's face. The bucket she held slipped from her grasp, sending ice chips skating across the floor.

"There you go," Walter said, and clapped her on the ear with the flat of his hand. Loretta staggered but Walter grabbed her by the arm and raised his hand again, but before he could bring it down, Clayton came up from behind and swung a wooden duck decoy to the back of Walter's head with such force the bird's head snapped from its body. Walter toppled in slow motion. On the way down, his forehead struck the corner of the countertop and blood began pooling from both wounds as soon as he settled to the floor. Clayton stood over him, still holding the duck head.

"Lord Jesus, what have you done?" Loretta said.

"Is he dead?"

"Go. Hurry"

"Come with me."

"Just go."

Clayton took his johnboat from the creek behind Sonny's ESSO out into the marsh, staying to the narrow cuts that power craft avoided. He imagined being hunted and felt confident he could avoid detection. But for how long, and to what end? He had navigated the waters around Sand Point since he'd been seven years old, and normally he loved being on the estuary, but today the still air held the odor of decay: rotting vegetation, marsh gasses seeping up through the mud. As the day wore on, a hazy sun dipped below a line of loblolly pine on the western horizon, and as dusk settled, a raccoon on the bank pinned and delicately disassembled a fiddler crab. A red-winged blackbird perched on a cattail, a vague presence in the fading light except for the blood-like slash on its wing. Full dark, Clayton turned the boat toward Sonny's gas station.

Sonny was at the kitchen table when Clayton entered. He pointed to a chair and set a beer on the table beside it.

"You heard?" Clayton asked.

Sonny nodded, drank from his beer. "Drove over there when the sheriff called for you. I guess the good news is you didn't kill the man."

Clayton pried the cap with the church key and tried to keep his hand from shaking as he sucked foam from the bottle lip. "I would not have wanted that on my conscience. But he was beating her."

"Not my business. Yours neither."

"It's wrong."

Sonny looked at Clayton straight on. "You don't have much claim on the moral high ground."

Clayton started to answer, and then turned his gaze downward, and his face reddened. So, Sonny knew.

"How bad off is he?"

"Said maybe a concussion. Wouldn't go to the hospital." Sonny drank and stifled a belch with the back of his hand. "Also said he would not bring charges. Said for you to see him in the morning before he changes his mind."

"Well, then. Good."

"I'll be going with you."

"No." Clayton finished his beer and stood. "Not your business, remember?"

WALTER WAITED AT THE DOOR when Clayton arrived just after sunrise. His head was wrapped in clean, white gauze and the side of his face was swollen. He smiled at Clayton as if he were welcoming a loyal customer. "Looks like another hot one, don't it?" He motioned Clayton in and shut the door. "You gave me a pretty good thump yesterday," Walter said with a laugh and a pat to his bandaged head. His joviality put Clayton immediately on guard. He kept within a step from the front entrance. He felt sweat at his armpits.

"Loretta is a nice girl, but a baby yet, still learning how to be a good wife," Walter continued conversationally, his tone free of edge or apparent anger. "But you are older. You should know better than to covet something that ain't yours."

Clayton forced down the growing panic, felt stupid for thinking a secret could be kept in a town small as Sand Point. Walter knew also, they all knew. All along? What an idiot he was.

Walter turned toward the back room. "Loretta, come on out here."

Loretta appeared from the living quarters, each step measured, her expression blank. She stopped beside Walter and looked down at the floor. Walter rested a hand on her shoulder, still smiling. Clayton's chest tightened, and he had to remind himself to breathe.

"Loretta, honey, you're my wife, ain't you?"

"I am."

"You want to keep it that way?"

"I do."

"You know it's my duty as husband to lead you, to show you right from wrong?"

"Yes, Walter." Walter looked directly at Clayton when Loretta spoke, smile calcified, and eyes hardened, sharp edged and glinting. It occurred to Clayton that he was watching a play.

Walter went around the counter and reached beneath it. Clayton instinctively, and as he later was to self-judge, cowardly, reached for the door, put his hand on the knob. A gun? Walter produced instead a worn leather razor strop, three inches wide, and two feet in length. Clayton let his hand drop from the knob.

Walter motioned with the strop and Loretta bent over the counter, lifted her shift above her hips, and braced herself on her elbows. She wore no undergarment.

Clayton started toward Walter, but Loretta jerked her face up and riveted Clayton in place with a fierce expression, a mixture of humiliation, anger, and determination. And something more, something that froze Clayton's heart. She was making a choice. Walter caressed her backside as if he were stroking his hound, then stepped back and brought the strap down once, again, again. Clayton jumped with the sound of leather on flesh. Loretta flinched and stifled a cry with each lash. Walter set the strap on the counter, came up close behind her, obscenely nudging, and looked at Clayton.

"You still around tomorrow, stop on by and we'll continue our lesson." His voice was cold, expressionless. "The day after, more of the same. How's that sound?" He smiled.

Clayton searched Loretta's eyes for some direction, but she gave no hope. He backed out of the market, and began running, running until his lungs heaved, stopping only to vomit onto the road, splattering his shoes, running until he knew he still lived, felt his heart protesting, running until he found himself at Sonny's. He gathered his clothes in his duffle, placed a note on the kitchen table, *I'm sorry for everything, sell my boat*, and he walked to the paved highway and stuck out his thumb. As he waited for a ride, he realized he'd not spoken a word at the market. Watched it all play out without uttering a sound. Caused all this pain for him, Loretta, Sonny, everyone, without a word of defense or apology or confession. He knew this day would stay with him for the rest of his life, and already he mourned that fact.

McKnight, Colorado, August 1955

FOR TWO MONTHS, Clayton wandered wherever hitchhiking carried him. His only intent was to escape the sea, the tidal pull of Sand Point and of Loretta. He'd stay in a town working day labor—humping furniture for moving companies, cleaning construction sites, washing dishes—until he had enough pocket money to move on.

One day, he was hitching beside the highway somewhere east of Sterling, Colorado when a Cadillac convertible slowed and pulled onto the shoulder. The man behind the wheel had a fifth of Jack Daniels wedged between his legs. His hair was long and wavy, reminding Clayton a little of one of those rock and roll stars, and he wore a white shirt studded with pearl buttons and a leather string tie clasped by a blue stone the size of a gull's egg. "You know how to drive?" he asked.

"I do."

"Could use a break." The driver twisted the cap onto the bottle and rolled over the stick shift into the passenger seat. "Point for Denver."

Clayton had never driven such a car, the red leather upholstery still holding the smell of newness, the sleek white body without mar or dent and gleaming in the early sun as he raced it across the high plains. The man was soon asleep in the passenger seat, head back, snoring, the bottle slipped to the floor. The radio faded in and out, blasting doo-wop, and for a while Clayton let go of memories and relaxed into the moment.

Nearing Denver, the mountains grew from the horizon like huge ocean swells. Summer, and whitecaps still topped the peaks. It occurred to Clayton that those mountains could swallow up a man. He came upon the city with its low, gray haze like coastal fog hanging over stockyards and office buildings, and he continued driving while the owner of the Cadillac slept on. An hour into the high country, the road pleated into a series of switchbacks and Clayton had to downshift to accommodate a logging truck creeping uphill. The whining of the truck's engine woke the man, who straightened in his seat, massaged his temples, and looked about. "Where the hell are we?"

"I don't know, exactly," Clayton said.

"Well, shit-fire, boy, we're in the mountains."

"I guess."

"Pull over. Pull over and get out."

The man executed a precarious U-turn and pulled away. Clayton followed a hawk's shadow across a talus slide and then started walking, but soon another logging truck appeared and gave him a lift. They descended pine slopes that soon opened into a long narrow valley cut by a middling stream with riffles and pools, and on either side of the stream cattle grazed in fields of yellow wildflowers and tall grasses. The eastern slope rising from the valley appeared stave-sided, as if a cancer had been gouged from it, but on the western side, a mountain peak rose dramatically and threw the main street of a small town in the distance into shadow. The trucker dropped Clayton at the first stop sign coming into McKnight, a three-block town holding, from what he could see as he walked, an assortment of small businesses: a tavern, a feed store, a coin laundry, a combination hardware and sporting goods store with a "Hunters Welcome" banner hanging over the entrance. From the side streets, three church steeples poked above the storefronts. Clayton paused outside a glass-fronted café, Nora's, and assessed his hunger against the few dollars in his wallet and the coins jingling in his pocket.

He entered Nora's. The lunch hour past, not yet time for the evening meal, the café was empty. Red vinyl booths lined the walls, three tables occupied the center space, and a counter separated the front of the room from the cooking area. Behind the counter, a woman was scraping down the grill top.

"Can I still get something to eat?" Clayton asked. The woman waved with her spatula toward the counter without turning. Clayton took a seat and studied the one-page mimeographed menu. The smell of frying hamburger and onion hung in the air.

"What can I get you?" The waitress placed a glass of water in front of him and leaned both hands on the counter. She appeared closing in on middle age, forty maybe, a few years either side, with a sturdy build, strong looking hands, corded forearms. A swath of dark hair streaked with gray hung down the side of her face.

"A grilled cheese, maybe. With tomato if you have it. And coffee."

"Fries?"

He calculated. "I guess not."

The woman tucked her hair behind her ear and walked to the grill and began to assemble his sandwich. Clayton rose and washed in the bathroom at the rear of the café and when he returned the grilled cheese was on the counter along with a platter of fried potatoes and a slab of berry pie. "Left over from lunch," the waitress said, thumbing through receipts by the cash register. "Just have to toss it if you can't eat it."

Clayton ate in silence, chewing slowly, a trick he'd learned traveling across country. Made a little seem like more. When the waitress came to refill his coffee, he looked up from his plate. "Are you Nora?"

"I am."

"Sign in your window says you could use help."

Nora regarded him. "Can you fry cook?"

"Not yet."

"Well, that's an honest answer. Drink?"

"I can't afford to drink much."

"You look to have ten fingers and ten toes. Why not get on with the survey or construction crews? Make a decent living."

"What are they surveying?"

Nora pointed to a map resting on an easel in one corner of the café.

"McKnight is living on borrowed time," she said. "The state plans a new reservoir. They come up from Denver every few months and give us updates from that map. The café will be thirty feet underwater in a few years."

"The whole town?" Clayton asked, glancing out the window on Main Street.

"The state's offered to relocate us, reincorporate a few miles downstream of the new dam. Some will accept, others not."

"You?"

"Don't know. Time yet to sort things out. Anyway," Nora returned to present business. "They're hiring and it's good work."

"I guess I'd rather fry cook," Clayton said. What he left unsaid was that he likely would not be around for long.

"Have it your way," Nora said. "Here, the pay's bad and the hours worse. We cater to the mine and the rancher schedules. And the construction crews lately. I close after the lunch hour on Saturdays and all day Sunday."

"That sounds fine by me," Clayton said. "Thanks." He stood and pulled a few wadded bills from his pocket. Nora shook her head. "Food comes with the job. Great benefits package here at Nora's."

Winter in the Valley, 1955

CLAYTON LIVED OUT THE SUMMER in a tent on the low slopes of Mount McKnight, the unscarred peak west of town. He had surprised himself for staying on as long as he had. Often during those first months he hiked the mountain to the summit overlook. To the west, the Rockies stretched out wave after wave beyond vision; to the east through a notch in the foothills the land flattened, a blue plain passing into infinity. The vastness reminded him of the sea, and oddly, he felt closer to home than anywhere he'd traveled since leaving Sand Point. He'd sit at the overlook awhile and bathe in its soul-soothing powers. Almost always, however, by association, Loretta Pine eventually would slip into his thought stream, and he would see her bent over the counter awaiting the strap and he would flush with shame and with longing, and he would hike back down from the mountain and go silent for a few days.

With the first snows of September, Nora put down a mattress on the floor of the storeroom and brought in a table, chair, and reading lamp. "It's not much," she motioned to the room, "but it's warm." She brushed a dried aspen leaf from Clayton's hair. "Don't want my fry cook frozen solid by a quick storm."

A stack of winter clothing lay folded on the table: long underwear, a pair of flannel trousers, and two sweaters.

"Thought you could use them," Nora said. "He was about your size."

"Your husband?"

She nodded. "He's a trucker. Loves to be on the road. One trip about four years ago now, he decided he wouldn't be coming back."

"Sounds like a hard man."

"Not at all," Nora said. "We loved each other once. Then we didn't. Nothing spiteful."

Clayton ran his hand along one sweater. "It's good you can be done with it and move on."

"Sometimes I feel sorry for myself," Nora said. "But that's no way to spend a life."

By December, weather swept into the valley, sealing it off from the world outside McKnight for days at a time. During the third week in January, a great storm blew in from the northwest, dumping snow measured in feet and driving it sideways by relentless winds. Clayton stood at the door of the diner and lost sight of the hardware store directly across the street. Road traffic slowed and then stopped altogether and by evening the town stood deserted. Sometime during the night, the power failed and the wind drifted snow over the café windows and blocked the door completely, leaving Clayton alone. Morning, he made coffee over the gas burner and sat bundled against the cold in one of the booths and read by the dim glow that filtered through the snowbanks. It was a place of exquisite exile so foreign that it seemed a different world entirely, a hibernation, and he could feel his blood slowing, his body suspended in a long, soft exhale, at peace, and when two days later he heard the road plows working outside, he already looked forward to the next blizzard.

Mid-February, a Saturday, sometime deep into the night, a sound brought Clayton groggily awake, and a voice.

"It's me."

"Is something wrong."

"Can I stay awhile?"

"Want me to make coffee?"

"No. I want to lie beside you. Would that be all right?" Something in Nora's tone would have made him agree to anything at all she asked.

"Yes." Clayton rolled onto his side, away from her, and listened to the rustle of her clothes falling away and felt the weight of her body lowered onto the mattress and the warmth of her length pressing against him. They rested there, silent, Clayton not sure what to do, until he thought perhaps she'd fallen asleep. But her hands began moving gently over him, stroking, probing, her tongue sampling his shoulder, and he came fully alive for the first time in months, and he turned to her.

Sunday morning, the café closed, Clayton stood at the stove making coffee and feeling conflicted, guilty about thinking of Loretta when he was with Nora, and uncertain what lay ahead. Presently, she appeared beside him.

"Coffee ready, eggs in a minute," he said.

"Nothing for me, I have to be going."

He faced her. "Last night," he began but fumbled where to take it.

Nora placed a hand on his arm. "Yesterday was one of those days that once meant a lot to me. I needed to be with someone, and I thank you."

So, perhaps Nora was thinking of someone else as well. "Anytime," Clayton said, stupidly. He felt like slapping his forehead.

"Enjoy your day off." Nora smiled, and left.

Summer, 1956

CLAYTON LASTED IN THE CAFÉ until spring took solid hold and he felt drawn to the outdoors, to the solitude of the pine slopes.

Nora must have sensed his restlessness. "Saw Hoyt McKnight the other day," she mentioned. "Said he's having a hell of a time finding help for the ranch."

Clayton knew Hoyt, son of the town's founder. He stopped at the café regularly, attended the reservoir meetings stone-faced, but otherwise seemed outgoing and someone the community looked to for leadership. Clayton had never spent much time talking with him, but Clayton never spent much time talking with anyone, not even with Nora, who, once begun, continued at irregular and widely spaced intervals to visit his storeroom.

"Seems like a fair man to work for," Clayton said from the grill. "But I wouldn't leave you without help."

"Look around," Nora said. "The dam is almost built. People are taking their buyout and moving on. Truth is, neither of us need help full time. You'd have room for both."

Mac gave Clayton the old foreman's cabin to stay in on the days he worked at the ranch. It was sided in unfinished planks, one room with a bed and a few pegs for clothes, a bare floor, and no plumbing. But Mac had run in electricity for lights, and the wood stove kept the cabin warm and the coffee hot.

On occasion, Mac had Clayton to the main house where they sat after dinner on the front porch to look out over the valley as night came on.

"I was born in this house in eighty-five," Mac said one evening. "Used to be you could sit right here and read by the Milky Way."

"I used to go out on the sand at night," Clayton said. "Sit and stare at the ocean, the moon off the water. It went on forever, endless. I sometimes get that same feeling here."

They both fell silent. A coyote sounded in the hills. Another answered. Mac pointed to the mountain, now purple against a lighter night sky. "This place used to be sea," Mac said. "I've found shell fossils and fish skeletons etched in the rock. It's the sea in these hills that drew you here."

Into the 1960s

ONE YEAR PASSED, and another, and on and on. Clayton settled into solitude as if born to it. Dinner, sometimes, with Mac; occasional visits from Nora during the night. Otherwise, he'd rather be alone in the woods or working Mac's fields than socializing in town. Seclusion felt safe. Every few months he's check in with Sonny, sometimes just to hear the accent of home. He never asked about Loretta, and Sonny never offered news of her. They talked of the water, mostly, of the striped bass that had disappeared from the bay and then returned, of crabbing, what a bushel was going for.

And then, one dark, sunless afternoon, mid-winter 1960, Walter Pine died. Sonny called Clayton at the café with the news.

"Stroke or some such," Sonny said.

"I appreciate the news," Clayton said. "I hadn't really thought about him in a long while."

There was silence on the line and Clayton thought they'd been disconnected.

"You don't usually lie to me," Sonny said. "It ain't a becoming trait."

And so. The news Clayton had been waiting for years to hear. And what of it? He hung up the phone after a few minutes and returned to the grill. Walter's death had no impact on Clayton's sense of shame.

A SWELTERING AFTERNOON in July of 1962, Clayton was mowing alfalfa when he noticed the sheriff's brown sedan pull into Mac's long drive, move slowly to the ranch house, and idle until Mac came out. Clayton continued mowing, but late in the day he noticed that Mac had hauled a trailer of hay bales around front and was barricading the road with them. Clayton left the mower in the field and joined him.

"No need for you to stay here," Mac said.

"Does this have to do with the sheriff?" Clayton asked.

"Final notice. They want to start the backfill."

Clayton had been aware of work on the reservoir winding down over the past months, but had not known Mac's property was one of the first in line for flooding.

They stacked bales three high across the drive in front of the house. Clayton wasn't sure why. To slow an assault? Mac had set a lever action western rifle conspicuously on top of one of the bales, and although a patrol car appeared at the ranch entrance from the county road, it sat idle. No one appeared in a rush to settle things.

They finished stacking and Mac went inside and returned with two beers and they sat on the porch as dusk settled. Mule deer moved from the pine slopes into the fields. They drank their beers as the deer faded into ghosts.

"I have a son and a daughter," Mac said. "Did you know that?"

"I believe you did mention it." To Clayton's knowledge, they'd never visited in the years he had been on the ranch.

"One in Phoenix, one in L.A. Know what they want me to do with the house?"

"No."

"Cut it right down the middle. Move it in sections up the hill there," he pointed. "Where the lakeshore will be after the reservoir is finished."

"What do you think?" Clayton asked.

"A dude ranch, they want. My daddy's homestead, a dude ranch." Clayton could hear the disappointment in Mac's voice. "I won't have it turned into a damned motel for rich folk to play cowboy."

"No, sir."

"And I sure as hell won't watch them bulldoze it." Mac breathed in the night air, and out. "Help me?"

"Yes, sir."

Mac walked to the truck and pulled two gas cans from the bed. They went inside and doused the stuffed chairs and the couch in the front room and the bedding upstairs. Mac opened the gas lines on the stove, and they went outside. Mac lit an oil rag and without hesitation tossed it through the front door. They drove to the foreman's cabin and sat in the cab of the pickup watching the fire lick from the windows until the gas stove blew with such a swoosh that flames shot from every opening and one side wall fell completely away.

Shortly thereafter, Nora accepted the Water Board's final buyout offer. Clayton packed the last of her boxes in the bed of her pickup and stood leaning against the cab. She'd wanted a few minutes alone in the cafe.

"Funny," she said, when she returned. "Without customers, without the smell of meals cooking, it doesn't feel that hard to walk away."

"That's good."

Nora opened the truck door and then turned and grabbed Clayton's arm. "Listen," she said. "I worry about you. Don't stay here. Whatever you are looking for, it's not here. Time for a new start. For both of us."

"I'll give it some thought," Clayton said.

"Don't think on it too long." She climbed behind the wheel and cranked the engine. "Look in the mirror. Neither of us is getting any younger." Clayton had turned thirty earlier that year.

Sand Point, September 1962

SAND POINT HAD CHANGED during Clayton's seven years away. He almost missed the turnoff from the state highway because a strip mall occupied what used to be a soybean field. He followed the narrow two-lane road leading toward the shore, asphalt now rather than gravel and crushed shell, and, rounding a curve, he came upon Walter Pine's fish market almost before he realized. It remained a part of the past, the same dirt parking lot, the same austere cinderblock exterior, except now painted a robin-egg blue with a red tin roof. He slowed, tightened his grip on the wheel, but kept going. The market was one reason he'd returned, but he could not will himself to stop, to find out who might still be there, who might be gone. He'd know soon enough.

Clayton drove to the south end of the beach where the cottages thinned. A squall was building out in the Atlantic, so he grabbed his poncho from the truck and walked south along the empty sand. The storm drew closer, the wind stiffening, lightening stabbing the ocean. Clayton burrowed into a dune and hooded himself with the poncho as the squall passed overhead in a swift, drenching, thunder-cracking charge. Afterwards, the ionized air smelled new and briny. The water settled oil-slick calm and reflected an iridescent green. Far out, a few shafts of sunlight broke from the clouds. Clayton rose from the dune feeling reborn and walked back to his truck to reunite with Sonny and to see about his boats and gear. He was grateful Sonny had not sold them.

CLAYTON GUIDED HIS BOAT along the tidal creek, checking his crab pots, harvesting his catch, neither as numerous as before, nor as large, but there still where he knew he'd find them. This is what he'd wanted for so many years, to be on the water. Squint-eyed, brown-skinned, sun-baked, alive on the water. He moored at Walter's old dock, harboring no expectations. He'd not yet shown himself to Loretta, although she most probably had heard of his return. Would she even care? What right had he? He unloaded his basket of crabs and passing the living quarters on his way to the storefront, a fluttering curtain caught his eye. There she was. He stopped, holding his basket like an offering. Loretta stood at the window motionless, expressionless. He felt the old yearning, an aching from somewhere inside that could only be called his soul. They regarded one another, and then she turned from the window and was gone.

Clayton continued around front and sat on the steps of the market. He did not try the door, did not enter. He sat on the stoop with his thoughts, his meditation floating in the humid southern air. Although just into his thirties, he regretted lost years, what might have been, a life lived one way rather than another, choices made and not made. But he was back on the water now, and a waterman he would remain, and he gave thanks for that. He felt the sun on his face, smelled the sea on the breeze, and heard the crabs scratching in his crate. He looked down at his hands, nicked by the wire of the traps, and by the sharp points of the shells. A waterman's hands. He sat there patiently, waiting for the door to open, or not.

THE LIES WE TELL OURSELVES

Loretta wakes when Clayton slips from bed and collects his clothes and moves on creaking steps downstairs. The wall opposite the window pulses with soft light as an easy offshore breeze flutters the curtains. A full moon, July. She knows the tide will run strong, a good fishing tide, and that he will be gone for a few days at least, maybe more. They've talked about how she needs him at the market. Time after time, they have had that conversation, beginning when their son, Dan, was born in 1965. The store brings in more cash in a month during the tourist high season in Sand Point than he can earn in half a year of fishing and crabbing. And, he's agreed that, yes, his help is needed, both in the store and with raising their son; those priorities should override his addiction to the sea.

He'd settle into a routine for a while—stocking shelves, cleaning storage rooms, painting and repairing whatever needed painting and repairing, dealing with suppliers, any task at all as long as it didn't involve visiting with customers. Clayton was not comfortable with casual conversation. But, always, after a month or two, Loretta would notice a mood come over him, like a junkie in withdrawal, a physical

25

longing she could see in his eyes and sense in the hesitant way he moved, and he'd be gone again to the ocean or to the bay or to the shack he'd built in among the scrub thickets blanketing the inshore sand dunes.

She rises when she hears the kitchen door shut, moves to the window and watches Clayton walk toward the storage shed to collect his gear. He's roused Dan and together they disappear into the shadows and reappear a few minutes later, each with an oar over one shoulder. A canvas knapsack hangs from Dan's other shoulder and Clayton carries a larger gear bag. At thirteen, Dan's growth spurt is raging. From a distance, in the dim light, it's difficult to tell them apart. They load the bags and oars in the bed of the pickup, climb in and pull away. The truck passes between two loblolly pines guarding the crushed shell driveway and onto the two-lane blacktop leading to the town a mile away. From there, they will leave the road and drive the hard-packed sand north for another mile to the section of land they bought cheaply years ago on the peninsula that dead ends at the swampy inlet where the sound empties into the ocean.

This is where Clayton keeps his skiff for setting his net in open water and his flat-bottomed johnboat for crabbing in the sound. Dan will help launch the boat and afterwards walk home to breakfast with Loretta. He'll return to Sand Point that evening, when he and Clayton retrieve the net and clean the catch and, if Clayton decides to remain the night, which he will, Dan will deliver the fish to the market. Clayton will fish from shore into the night until he grows weary and then sleep in the truck or in a nest scooped from a dune, with a tarp for cover should rain threaten. He'll show up a few days or a week later, revived, scraggly-bearded, a bit sheepish, perhaps, and prepared to engage with civilization again, at least for a while. Loretta's sick of it all. She's sacrificed so much for what she has, the busy market, a little money in the bank.

Later, downstairs, Loretta brews coffee and scrambles eggs. When Dan arrives, she puts two pieces of bread in the toaster and pours him milk. "Wash up," she says, pointing to the kitchen sink. Dan splashes his face and makes a pass with the soap over his hands. He sits and drains his glass in one long pull and she refills it. He shovels egg onto a piece of toast and eats it and washes it down with the milk. Since spring, it's been impossible to fill him, or, for that matter, to keep him properly dressed. His trousers end above his ankles and he's outgrown two pairs of sneakers before they show any wear at all.

"Rinse the dishes when you're finished," Loretta says. "I have to open."

"I'll come with you," Dan says.

"You get a little more sleep. Come over after you rest and shower." She appreciates his offer. Their son does not share his father's reclusive personality. He's outgoing, an asset in the store. He and Loretta make a good team: they upsell with ease.

"That's a lovely little piece," she might comment about a small watercolor seascape that catches the eye of a tourist. "But, have you seen this?" and Dan would bring out a canvas-back duck decoy hand-carved from a single block of juniper, hand-painted, and priced at three times the watercolor. "An old man from Currituck brought it in just yesterday," Dan would say. "Said his granddaddy made it way back when."

Loretta leaves Dan at the kitchen table mopping the last of the eggs with the second piece of toast. She walks the quarter-mile to the store, Walter's Market, a tin-roofed, square cinderblock building that fell to her, along with the

strip of beachfront Clayton loves, following her first husband's death, eighteen years earlier, in 1960. Walter Pine was
grieved neither by Loretta nor by anyone who knew him,
but she retained the store's name because folks were used
to it. She painted the roof a Cardinal red and changed the
outside wall color every few years to suit her whim—laurel
green, teal, baby blue, and currently, periwinkle. Over the
years, although she kept the fresh fish counter and the cold
drink case, she phased out most of the dry goods to make
space for fine art, local crafts, and an assortment of beach-
themed junk—oyster shell ashtrays, dishtowels stenciled
with seagulls, inflatable tubes and rafts.

At the market, she unlocks the front door, steps inside, and
relocks it. It's the quiet part of the morning, early yet, and she's
not quite ready for business to commence. Clayton's latest
abandonment has put her in a reflective mood, to consider how
far she's come over the years, with him at times, but mostly
without. She runs her hand along the smooth wooden surface
of the checkout counter on which sits an antique cash register,
eyes the display racks, the pantry, assessing stock, and then
wanders to the rear of the store. A door leads to the back rooms
where she and Walter once lived. Although she's redecorated
the front of the store, she's kept the living space much as it
was when they first moved there in 1950, he already exiting
middle age, she barely into her teens. The door opened into
one plain room, a central living area containing an overstuffed
chair, a sofa, and a small, round dining table on which sat a
Philco midget Bakelite radio. A kitchen area was to one side
of the living area, and to the other side a bathroom with a
cold-water shower separated two bedrooms large enough
only to hold a twin bed and a three-drawer chest. So spare,
but at the time, even with Walter's aged mother living with

them for the short time before her death, the quarters had seemed spacious.

Loretta hears Dan calling and returns to the front of the market to find him at the cooler taking out a bottle of orange soda. "I thought you were going to sleep," she says. "Couldn't." Dan flips the bottle cap and tastes the soda. He cocks his head, listens, and smiles. "Customers." Loretta notices him check his reflection in the display case glass, remove a black comb from his pocket and run it through his hair, take another drink from the bottle, and wipe his mouth with the back of his hand. It's the first time she's seen him use a comb. He's on the verge, she thinks, and worries about the competing tugs between her world and Clayton's.

LORETTA WILLIAMS WAS BORN in Kings Corner, North Carolina, in either 1934 or 1935. There was some debate as to exactly when the eldest of the eleven children came into the world. Dates got mixed after around the fifth or sixth child. Her father, Johnny Williams, remembered her arriving on December 28th, but her mother, Elizabeth, insisted it was January 3rd, and most everyone trusted her memory as she was the one to go through twenty hours of labor while he spent the day and maybe the one after drinking homebrew with his pals.

Elizabeth suffered some sort of mental fatigue following Loretta's birth, and there were no brothers or sisters around the house for several years. But just after her sixth birthday, the others began arriving in bunches, and Elizabeth required Loretta's help in raising them. While other girls played after school by the creek or took turns braiding one another's hair, Loretta was expected home promptly. Her youngest siblings, two sets of twins back to back, were still suckling when Loretta began high school.

Johnny was a hard worker whose hard drinking sometimes got in the way of steady employment. Although a man who took pride in his children, he failed at times to provide for them. At Elizabeth's urging, Pastor Roy stopped by one evening after Johnny had lost his latest job for getting into a drunken brawl with his foreman after work.

"You know, Johnny," the pastor counseled, "drink can be a hard master if you allow it."

Johnny lowered a wet rag from his swollen right eye. "Didn't realize he was a lefty." He let the pastor stew with confusion for a second or two and then continued. "Our Lord's first miracle was turning water into wine." And, before the pastor could respond, "That ought tell a man all he needs to know about drink." Johnny was functionally illiterate, but inherited from his mother a passing knowledge of the Bible that he distorted to his advantage when confronted with his shortcomings.

Like that time the clucking women dropped off laundry for Elizabeth, muttering under their breath about him, wondering why a man whose unstable work history forced his wife to take in wash would continue to produce offspring like a breed bull. Johnny had shut them up as they passed. "Psalm 127, blessed is the man whose quiver is full of children," he misquoted. When they glanced his way, he fiddled with his belt buckle. "And I got me a full quiver."

When Loretta was fourteen, the earth swallowed up her father. Johnny had been hired day labor on a sewer project, ditching and laying pipe. He'd gone to work deeply hungover and was napping during the lunch break in the shade at the bottom of the trench when the soil pile, positioned too close to the sidewall, backfilled. At first, no one noticed Johnny missing, but when the crew discovered the collapsed trench and a pair of boots projecting from the dirt mound, they disinterred him, pounded on his back, flushed the soil from his nose and mouth, and succeeded in getting him breathing. Barely. They carted him home and into bed and Elizabeth sat with him during the night, waiting for him to die, or to recover.

Turns out, he did neither. He survived, but was permanently addled. He lost the names of his children, communicated in nonsense, and spent a good portion of most days sitting on the porch stoop whittling with a dull jackknife a stick one of the children would fetch for him each morning. Loretta dropped out of school to help look after her younger brothers and sisters while her mother nursed Johnny and continued with her piecemeal laundry. Loretta was observant and quick to master the basic skills required to run a household: the cleaning, cooking, sewing, gardening, canning, and on and on. But always, the family lacked: for food, for decent clothing, for shoes that fit, for coal. At times, a sack of potatoes or bag of greens would show up on the porch. Elizabeth always waited until full dark before sending one of the children out to retrieve the charity. Loretta tried never to be the one chosen.

When it appeared Johnny would get no better, Loretta went to work part-time at the local grocery. Walter Pine, the owner, was deep into his fifties and possessed a gut that required energy to haul around. He hired her on delivery days to help offload the truck and restock the shelves. Far sturdier than her slight frame implied, Loretta made herself useful hauling sacks of rice and onions, unloading crates of produce, boxes of canned goods. Walter was known as a hard boss, and she sensed him keeping a close eye on her, so she made a point never to show fatigue, even when bone-tired from spending the night tending to a croupy sibling or from helping her mother with the wash.

One day, when she had been working at the store for six months, Walter Pine approached her as she was finishing her shift. He set a cloth-wrapped country ham on the counter.

"How old are you?"

Loretta tucked a loose strand behind her ear. "Fifteen. Almost."

"What's almost, girl?"

"Two months shy."

Walter thrummed his fingers on the counter and was silent for long enough to cause Loretta to fidget, and finally he slid the ham across the counter and nodded to her. "For your mama. Tell her I'll stop by this evening to have a word." Walter Pine was not known for his generosity, even though he owned the market outright and collected rent on several other properties around town. When he occasionally did extend credit or contribute to some cause or another, he expected recognition. The thought of him offering her mother a ham filled her with dread. She tucked it in the crook of her arm and walked home fearing Mr. Pine was going to let her go. She tracked back through her day, and the only thing she could recall was that he had called, "Careful there," when she had stumbled carrying a flat of eggs. Could that have been cause enough?

That evening, a rapping at the door caused Loretta to stiffen and tuck herself into a dark corner.

"Hello, Elizabeth." Walter Pine stepped across the threshold but moved no farther into the house. He glanced about, acknowledging neither Loretta nor Johnny nor the clutch of children scooting about underfoot. Loretta suddenly saw the room not as her home, but as the shanty it was—overcrowded, roughly furnished, and dank with the odors of overdue diapers, collards stewing on the stove, and a vague stench of decay coming off her father. "Might I have a word with you?" he asked Elizabeth. "On the porch?"

They stepped outside and Loretta inched close to the door but could not follow the conversation, consisting mostly of the low rumbling of Mr. Pine's voice with the occasional response from her mother. After a period of silence, Loretta cracked open the door and chanced a peek outside. Mr. Pine was nowhere to be seen, and her mother sat on the front step with her face in her hands. Loretta went outside and sat beside her.

"Oh, Mama, he fired me, didn't he?

Elizabeth raised her head from her hands. Her eyes glistened.

"Mama, I'm so sorry. I don't know what I did wrong."

Elizabeth straightened, smoothed her dress over her lap, and took a deep breath. "No, child. He did not fire you. He wants to wed you."

Loretta stared dumbly at her mother, as if she spoke in tongues. Elizabeth explained Walter Pine's offer. A recently minted widower, he needed someone to help with his aging mother, and to cook and clean for him. She did not mention the rest, what more would be expected. Loretta listened without comprehending, the words buzzing around her ears like a swarm of flies. The speaking finally stopped, and Loretta sensed her mother waiting for a response.

"What do you want me to do, Mama?"

"I only want what's best for you," Elizabeth said, but went on to mention that there would be a little money coming from Mr. Pine each month, "to make up for taking your help away."

"You would have an entire house to yourself," Elizabeth finished. "Just you and Mr. Pine and his mother. Imagine."

So, Loretta realized. It had been decided.

There was no honeymoon. Nothing of the sort. Loretta had never kissed a boy, let alone done what Mr. Pine demanded of her that first night together when he led her by the hand to bed and lifted her nightdress and rolled on top of her, his bulk suffocating, his breath rancid and gag-inducing, and below, his pumping and probing. She felt a brief sharp pain but really had been struggling so for breath, she later had no notion of him inside her, if in fact he'd found what he'd been poking for, other than noticing the dampness on the bedsheet, and a bit of blood mixed with his expulsions.

Loretta was too numb and cowed those first days to do anything but cook and clean and avoid Walter Pine for as many hours a day as possible. For his part, although stern with her, Walter seemed pleased with his new possession. Often, he'd come near and stroke her hair, pat her hip, step back and appraise her as if admiring a prized hound he'd recently acquired. And, his appetites! He ate more during one meal than her family often had for a day. He tallied the earnings from the store daily, stacking the dollars and coins on the dining table, grunting with greed, jotting totals on a pad, growing aroused by the numbers, pointing Loretta to the bedroom.

Walter Pine's mother hardly spoke, and then to him only. A ghostly presence, dressed always in a black mourning gown, she spent her days shuffling through the house or sitting on the sofa working her mouth as if chewing cuds and staring at the wall, or at a page from the *Saturday Evening*

Post that Mr. Pine ordered weekly to keep her company. She'd be in bed by sundown.

On the ninth day of Loretta's new life, as Walter left for the market, he instructed Loretta to hurry with Mrs. Pine's breakfast and get to the store. It was delivery day. Loretta overcooked Mrs. Pine's soft-boiled egg, watched it bounce from her slotted spoon onto the plate, rubbery and hard. When she set it with the toast on the table, the old woman made an indistinct sound.

"Beg pardon," Loretta said and leaned close, straining to hear.

"Harlot," Mrs. Pine hissed.

Loretta left the old woman with her egg and toast and went into the bedroom, packed the few possessions she'd brought with her, and walked home. At the stoop, she hesitated, thought of knocking at the door, wondered if she still belonged. Less than two weeks gone, but she felt she'd aged a decade. She did not knock. Inside, she found Elizabeth and Johnny and the two next oldest siblings at the table. A pleasant aroma filled the room, and their plates were full—biscuits with sausage gravy, slabs of fried ham, coffee, and milk for the children. They hardly ever had meat. Loretta temporarily was struck dumb. "Hi sister," two siblings said in unison, and went back to eating.

"Another of Mr. Pine's hams," her mother said by way of greeting, and perhaps apprehending her daughter's silence. "And money came in for coffee and whatnot. Are you hungry?" Her eyes fell to the satchel in Loretta's grip.

"I can't, Mama."

Elizabeth hesitated, glanced at Johnny, who was awaiting another forkful of sausage biscuit. She lifted it to his mouth and he chewed noisily. "Marriage takes some getting used to."

"The things he," Loretta began but stopped when her mother turned away and began fiercely slicing at the ham steak on her plate. The youngest set of twins began squawking from the corner. Diapers needed changing. "Life ain't easy anywhere," Elizabeth said, and started to rise.

"I'll take care of them," Loretta said, motioning her mother back to the chair. She changed the diapers, picked up her satchel, and went to the door. "I'll see you," Loretta said, but wondered if she ever would. Leaving, she sensed her past life shedding from her body like a heavy coat dropping to the ground, taking with it her hopes and dreams, and she continued on, surrendering the shell of what remained to a shadowy future.

The strop came out for the first time that night.

"Left dishes unwashed, late to work, I know where you went," Walter said when he returned from the market that evening. He went to the bathroom and returned with his leather razor strop. "You saw your kin with food on the table. Where do you think that came from?"

Loretta stared at the strop Walter held. He slapped it against the table, a heavy whacking sound. "You're a hard worker," he went on. "A fine-looking child, can't cook a lick, but you'll pick it up. You'll learn how to be a good wife. I'm here to teach you."

Loretta willed herself elsewhere, felt herself evaporating. Walter motioned her to the table, and almost gently guided her, positioned her elbows on the tabletop, bent at the waist. He went behind her and lifted her dress. Loretta faced Mrs. Pine, who watched from the sofa. Walter raised his arm and brought the strop across Loretta's exposed buttocks. Loretta's eyes went wide with pain, and surprise. Another lash brought her back fully into herself, and she gasped. Mrs. Pine cackled. Loretta's face reddened with humiliation.

"Let's not make a habit of this," Walter said, returning the strop to its hanging peg in the bathroom.

Three months later, at supper, Walter announced that he'd purchased a market up north, just over the Virginia state line, in a place called Sand Point. A larger market, a growing town. "Kings Corner has seen its best times."

"I don't want to go," Mrs. Pine said. It was the most she'd uttered in front of Loretta since they'd been together under one roof.

"Then, stay," Walter said, neutrally.

To her surprise, Loretta found herself looking forward to the move. She was weary of the sideway glances in her direction at church, the downward eyes of the customers at the store. Pity? Judgment? She was tired of the pull of her family home, her brothers and sisters. If absence really does make the heart grow fonder, maybe she could stop hating her mother.

And, surprisingly, Walter's Market in Sand Point allowed her a degree of freedom not available in Kings Corner. With living quarters in back of the store, whenever the claustrophobic presence of Walter or Mrs. Pine, who, in the end did go to Virginia, closed in on her, she could wander alone through the store, sit quietly in the ice room on hot days, walk the road without drawing notice.

LORETTA AND DAN SPEND the morning greeting customers. The locals come for fresh fish, crabs, and oysters when available. The tourists buy seafood as well, but also the high margin items—souvenir ashtrays and hand towels, T-shirts imprinted with stupid beach slogans, "I Caught Crabs in Sand Point," homespun handcrafts, and artwork. At noon, she sends Dan home for lunch. He asks if she would like something brought back for her and she declines. She's taken one of those pep pills and is not hungry. She's fallen into a habit during the busy season. A pill to get her going in the morning, revved up for the day, and one to settle her down for the night. She looks forward to both, and is a little worried about that, but not enough worried to cut back.

Dan returns just after one with a sandwich Loretta had not asked for but nibbled at nonetheless. He helps in the market until four, tracking his sales in a small ledger he keeps in a drawer at the checkout counter. He loves the sale, Loretta knows, loves the game like other boys love baseball, and each Sunday she makes a show of slipping him a few dollars "commission."

At four, Dan goes home to change into his fishing clothes—ragged jeans and ratty T-shirt—to help Clayton haul the net, and sort and clean the catch. When Dan leaves, Loretta debates phoning Arthur. Loretta met Arthur two years earlier. He and his wife and two girls spend two weeks mid-season at their vacation home, and another two weeks late, just before Labor Day. Twice a week or so, Arthur drops by Walter's Market late in the afternoon to shop for dinner and to burn time looking over her merchandise and chatting until cocktail hour. He's a realtor from one of the D.C. suburbs with a larger-than-life personality. The way he closes the distance between them when he comes into the market, the way he locks eyes with hers when they speak, Loretta knows he wants sex. It will never happen, she's not attracted to his type, the even tans, the soft hands, and the soft paunches, but she plays along with Arthur because he's offered to help her. At the end of last season, he suggested that she think about expanding.

"I've noticed this place does really well," he said. "Ever think about going big?"

"I don't think Sand Point is ready for much other than this," she said.

"Not here. Ocean City. Booming. I have contacts, could keep an eye out for opportunities."

"Move from here?" She knew Ocean City would be an easy drive for him. A day trip, for work, he could say, to avoid having to haul his family with him.

"Keep the options open," he said.

Loretta picks up the phone and dials Arthur's number, but when one of his daughters answers, she hangs up.

Business is steady and before she realizes it, it's already past six and she notices Dan coming into the parking lot pulling a red wagon holding the day's catch in a Styrofoam cooler. She helps him carry the cooler into the market and together they lay out the fish in the display case—spot, croaker, a few flounder and Spanish mackerel.

"Long day for you," Loretta says, when they are finished.

"Dad needs more ice," Dan says, and goes to the ice room to refill the cooler. Loretta follows.

"He could have come with you and taken it back himself."

"Crabbing on the bayside," Dan says. "I don't mind. It won't take long."

"That's not the point," Loretta says, but drops it.

She closes the market at seven and walks home in the softening light, thinking about Arthur's offer. The market has been so much of her life, but it holds as many bad memories as good. When Walter had been alive, she had been dead. When he died, she was reborn. But, in fairness, Walter had shown her that money, what she inherited from him, could buy, if not love or happiness, some level of comfort. The prospect of earning more in a new and larger setting excites her, and also frightens her, the upending of her safe, if routine existence. But, of course, Clayton will not be a part of that new life. She knows he will never leave Sand Point.

CLAYTON, HER FIRST LOVE. In the summer of 1950, she'd arrived in Sand Point with Walter and his mother, and when the market had been open a few days, a boy came through the door as she was ladling ice chips into the seafood display. He appeared near her age, maybe a bit older, and had a lean, hard frame.

"Can I help you?" she asked.

"Came to see Mr. Pine." He removed his cap, ringed it in his hands. "Business."

"Mr. Pine is out back, seeing to some repairs to the dock." She returned to her ladling, while he stood there watching. When she finished, she straightened and regarded him openly. His face reddened and he looked away. "You could go out back to see him."

"Pardon?"

"Mr. Pine. Out back, by the dock."

"Right," he said and backed toward the door. "Clayton," he said. "That's my name."

Loretta couldn't help but smile. "Loretta," she said.

Clayton, at eighteen already a known waterman in the area, sold Walter crabs. During his deliveries, she noted Clayton physically struggling to overcome his natural shyness to visit with her, and she encouraged him because she craved companionship with someone close to her age. Clayton was the only boy Walter allowed near, and then only to unload his baskets and to store the crabs in the ice room. But, over time, they managed to communicate with their eyes and in whispers when Walter was near, and, eventually, with their bodies when he was absent.

Their meetings went on for a few years, but it couldn't last. There are no secrets in a town the size of Sand Point. It was on a hot summer afternoon. Walter had business in Pungo and Loretta and Clayton had just made love in the ice room, all the while listening for customers. Still entwined, they heard the screen door creak open and slam shut. "Loretta."

"What?" Clayton started.

"Shush," Loretta said. She smoothed her shift and Clayton crouched behind the door.

"Stay here until he goes into the back room," Loretta whispered. She ladled a bucket of ice and carried it out front.

"Mr. Pine," she said. "I thought you were headed to Pungo?" She tried to keep her voice from trembling. Clayton's scent was on her still, the taste of his skin on her tongue, her face flushed from sex.

"Truck quit on me. Had to walk back in this goddamned heat."

"Let me get you some water."

"Bring me a beer."

"I don't believe we have beer. Lemonade?"

"There's beer. Find it."

"I can't find what's not there." She fought to keep her voice calm. She knew Walter teetered on the edge of violence.

Walter jabbed a finger in her face. "Watch that mouth."

Loretta flinched and the bucket slipped from her hand. Ice chips scattered.

"There you go," Walter said, and clapped her on the ear with the flat of his hand.

Through the pain, Loretta actually felt relief to have an excuse for her blushed complexion and flustered behavior. Walter grabbed her arm and raised his hand.

"No!" Loretta screamed, but not at Walter. Behind her, Clayton advanced, a wooden decoy held like a club. He struck Walter on the head and Walter toppled like a felled pine. Blood showed on the floorboards.

"Lord Jesus," Loretta said.

"Is he dead?" Clayton asked. He held the duck's head; its body lay at his feet, snapped off by the blow.

"Go."

"Come with me."

"Go."

Loretta gathered spilled ice in a dusting cloth and placed it under Walter's head. Walter moaned. She went to the telephone on the checkout counter and dialed the sheriff's office and asked for help. An accident, she explained. A fall. The sheriff arrived with the ambulance. The volunteer firemen wrapped his head, checked for concussion, and then Walter had a word with the sherriff in the back room.

Later, when Walter explained evenly that there would be no charges filed and that he'd sent word for Clayton to stop by to settle things, Loretta sensed what was to come. She knew Walter, and Walter knew her. She would be put to the test, and, as much as she hated herself for it, she knew her answer. The hundred dollars Walter slipped her each month to send to her family gave her a power she'd never experienced before. With Walter's mother long dead, she had few responsibilities other than to the store and to Walter, and, thank God, his cravings had eased with age and he often retired early. She had entire nights to herself to listen to the radio, to roam the front of the store free and easy, to sneak into the second bedroom for a peaceful rest.

The following morning, Loretta watched from the back room as Walter motioned Clayton into the market, shut the door, and posted the "Closed" sign in the window. When he called to her, Loretta emerged and stood beside Walter, never taking her eyes off Clayton.

"You my wife?" Walter asked.

"I am," Loretta said.

"You want to keep it that way?"

The test. She knew what was coming, knew Clayton had no idea. It was the price she'd pay to keep the cash flowing to her family, to realize the relative comfort of a bed rather than the roll-out mat that was hers back home, and the opportunity to learn a business that, because of Walter's age, she knew one day would be hers.

"I do," she answered.

A look of desperation came into Clayton's eyes and for a moment she weakened. Her body already ached for him again. But she began willing herself away, to another place, a place where pain did not exist, and Clayton's presence began to fade from her vision. "I do," she repeated, and saw Clayton physically slump.

Walter reached under the counter and brought out his razor strop. He bent Loretta over the counter, raised her shift, and administered the punishment. Clayton jerked with each stoke from Walter as if it were him being beaten. Loretta sensed humiliation and shame rise from him like an odor. But she felt no compassion. She was not present. She had removed herself to another place, a place where nothing could hurt her, a place free of want and urging and passion of any kind.

Walter finished, set the strop aside, and lowered Loretta's shift almost gently. He turned to Clayton. "You still around tomorrow, stop on by and we'll continue our conversation. The day after, more of the same."

Clayton hesitated at the door searching Loretta's face for any sign of hope, and seeing none, ran. That was the last Loretta saw of Clayton for more than seven years. Then, one day several months after Walter's second stroke had landed him in the ground, there he was, passing by her bedroom window carrying a basket of crabs.

DAN'S NOT HOME WHEN Loretta arrives from the market. Clayton often keeps him late on days when fishing is good, so she doesn't worry until she's finished frying a couple of hamburgers and roasting potato wedges for them, and still, Dan has not arrived. Full dark, she walks onto the porch and calls his name but in response hears only the shrill racket of tree frogs. At nine o'clock, she grabs a flashlight from the front closet and walks to the beach and from there toward the north end where Clayton keeps his boats. She finds them sitting in the sand beside a driftwood fire, eating Vienna sausages from the can and crackers from the box. She approaches, stands above them, waiting. Dan stares into the fire, looking, to Loretta, miserable. His left hand is bandaged with white gauze.

"Dan, what happened?"

"Just a slip with the bait knife," Clayton says. "Cleaned it up."

"What are you still doing here?" she continues, speaking to Dan. "You had me worried."

"I need to get the net out by three this morning," Clayton says. "I thought it would be better for him to stay here."

Now, she faces Clayton. "Without telling me?"

"It's OK," Dan says. "I don't mind."

"I thought we'd gig some flounder," Clayton says. "Catch a few hours sleep at the shack."

"I do," Loretta says. "I do mind." At the anger in her voice, Dan looks up pleadingly, and Loretta senses how torn he must feel.

Clayton stands, faces Loretta. "I'm sorry about not checking with you first. But I can't be sorry about what I do. That would be the end of me."

Loretta listens to Clayton, absorbs the truth of it, nods, and turns her back to the fire and to him. For a moment, she is filled with spite. They are standing on her property. Hers! Her rightful inheritance for enduring Walter for those awful years.

WALTER'S SECOND STROKE IN 1963, the bad one, affected his right side. His movements were uncoordinated and jerky, the right leg seeming at times to move in opposition to his left, the right arm limp and floppy at his side. But in slurred speech he continued to order Loretta around and became incensed when she failed to understand him, or worse, when she ignored him and went about the business of running the market. When he attempted to impose his will, to reach for her with his left hand in slow motion, she simply stepped away.

One evening Walter took to bed early, exhausted, and promptly pissed himself. He called to Loretta. "Change."

Loretta pulled his wet boxers from him.

Then, she went to the bathroom and brought out the strop.

She stood over him until he seemed to recognize her intent and then she brought the strop down across his naked thighs, again and again, until her arm tired and she saw first anger, and then pain register on his slack face. She straightened, her breath coming in heaves, and she waited for the emotions to overtake her, a sense of satisfaction or guilt or revenge or justice. But, she felt none of those things. She felt empty, diminished. She felt as though she'd killed something of herself. Her burden had not lightened, but intensified.

And then, Clayton returned. The sight of him on the porch of the market with his basket of crabs filled her with memories, and with memories, came yearning. She went to him, and without speaking, led him by the hand into the ice room.

They married right away, as if to make up for lost time, before either really had a chance to absorb how the other had changed during their years apart. Eventually, however, the distance between them became apparent. Before Walter's death, his growing list of infirmities kept him in the back room most days, and Loretta grew increasingly confident running the store, and after he died, she blossomed. Clayton, on the other hand, had become more withdrawn over time. His natural shyness, endearing during their youth, had deepened into occasional periods of tight-lipped withdrawal.

For a while, their lovemaking was enough to bind them. But, Loretta sensed something off even there. Clayton's touch, once urgent, became tame and uncertain, as if he were handling delicate china, or a fragile heirloom to which he had no right. Sometimes, it seemed as though Walter's ghost loomed.

Dan came along in 1965, and they moved from the market to a brick colonial just down the road, and although Loretta cherished their child, she determined not to fill the house with siblings. She'd not replicate for Dan her own childhood.

As Loretta began putting her touches on Walter's Market, replacing dry goods and snack foods with higher end merchandise, as she began promoting the market to the tourists, the freshest fish and crabs in town, the oysters and clams for seaside bakes, business surged, especially during the summer months. Clayton continued his crabbing and fishing, but there was no way he alone could keep the market stocked, and Loretta more and more depended on the wholesalers. Within a few years, Clayton's contribution to the market was more symbolic than helpful. The old ways. He was a waterman. She required a merchant.

LORETTA WALKS A FEW YARDS from the fire and waits for her anger to lift. She stares into the middle distance, and, for a moment, lights dotting the night like lightning bugs mesmerize her. Beach houses. Dozens of beach houses sitting atop the line of sand dunes looking out over the ocean. Over the years, investors had been purchasing beachfront property and dividing it into lots and filling those lots with expensive year-round homes.

It's impossible, and useless, to stay angry with Clayton for long. He's always been exactly the man he says he is. She decides at that moment that the developers will not get her oceanfront. She will never take this from Clayton. He will keep his shack and this strip of sand for as long as he wants it. But, his time is passing into history; she imagines it evaporating like morning dew. And as his world shrinks, hers swells with possibility, and she realizes now how desperate she is to bring Dan fully into hers. His constant moving between the two is confusing. He's of both of them, and wants to please his father, but he's not a natural loner—she pays attention to how he acts when no one is watching—joking with his friends, visiting with customers, bantering shyly with the girls he's begun to notice, and then going quiet around Clayton, mimicking his father's reserve.

Loretta returns to the fire, collected. "We'll talk tomorrow," she says to Clayton, or to Dan, or to both. She leaves them beside the fire and fades into the darkness beyond the reach of the flames. During her return walk, the night stills. Sweat dampens her underarms and trickles between her breasts. Crickets chirp from the roadside drainage ditch. It's almost eleven when she arrives at the house, and she has to open the market by seven the following morning, but she's not ready for sleep. She undresses, cools herself with a wet cloth, slips into her nightdress, and swallows a pill from the bottle she keeps on her nightstand. She lies in bed and scrolls through her future. She'll deed the peninsula property to Clayton, and he will be content. She will sell the market and the house, and use the proceeds to open a high-end shop in Ocean City, Loretta's Boutique, and will achieve both contentment along with wealth. Dan will thrive there and at the time of her choosing take ownership of the Boutique. This is the story she tells herself as she closes her eyes and feels the pill gently ease her toward sleep.

UNCLE BILLY'S BAR & GRILLE

Clayton finished his beer and dropped it in the stern where it pinballed against the other two empties when he veered the boat into the channel leading from the salt bay to the dock behind the market. He unloaded his crabs and carried the bushel baskets into the market and left them in the walk-in cooler. On his way out he glanced around the store. The layout was pretty much the same as when he and Loretta had owned it, except that the shelves that used to hold the high-end, handmade local crafts that Loretta loved now held the cheaper, mass-produced mementos that tourists favored over the more expensive alternatives. The new owners were busy with customers, so he lifted a hand in greeting and left. They would pay him later and pay him what he asked. The husband and wife were locals and knew he charged fairly and probably felt pity for him and never questioned his invoices.

Leaving the dock, Clayton guided his johnboat to the narrow finger of land he owned that jutted between the salt marsh on the east and the ocean on the west. He pulled the boat far up into the slip he'd carved years ago from the cat-tails and marsh grasses, tied off to the rotting bulkhead, and stepped off onto yielding lowland and walked the gentle rise to his cottage on firmer ground. He left his rubber boots on the porch, stripped off his weatherproof yellow bib overalls, and hung them on a peg inside the back door. He considered a shower. The flannel shirt and jeans he wore under his overalls retained the stench of sweat, crab bait, and swamp mud, but he could not muster sufficient interest so instead put on his wool cap and set out for Uncle Billy's Bar & Grille, a mile-and-a-half inland. During his walk, evening settled, the early October breeze carried a damp chill, and Clayton realized the crabbing season was coming to an end. He had no inclination to set winter pots, such meager returns, and no desire at all to sign on with one of the dredgers, the large workboats that rooted crabs from the sand where they buried to rest until spring. A time for everything, he reasoned, a time to harvest and a time to leave the crabs be. But the thought of another winter without Loretta and Dan put him in foul spirits. Although when they were together, he had cherished the solitary times when he left them to run the store so he could spend days on end at the cottage fishing and crabbing, he'd grown accustomed to returning to a settled family. The lifestyle suited his temperament, but obviously not Loretta's. It was six years ago, 1978, a good crabbing season. Sand Point was beginning to attract greater numbers of year-round residents, and high demand for the big Jimmies propped up prices. Clayton spent more time than usual working from the cottage and when he returned home one evening, about this time of year, he found the house empty and a note from Loretta. She'd left the deed to the cottage property for Clayton, and she'd kept the deeds to the home and the market. Both would sell quickly.

As he approached Billy's, Clayton paused, debating whether to enter. He'd forgotten it was a Friday, days never much registered with him, payday, and more than the usual assortment of dented pickups occupied the dirt lot. Billy's was nothing but a glorified fish shack, shot-and-a-beer type of place tucked in a clearing of loblolly pine. A yellow neon sign hanging above the door advertised not the establishment but its attraction: "Beer Here." A deep fryer for the fish, a flattop for the hamburgers, a rack for potato chips and beer nuts, a three-tap beer dispenser, a jukebox, pinball machine, a half-dozen tables, and a twelve-stool bar, that was it. No room for a pool table.

Clayton went inside. The regulars, the roofers, construction workers, and road crews knew him as the oddball who sat at the end of the bar, keeping to himself, having little to say to anyone. Of indeterminate age, they speculated, between forty-five and sixty depending on whom you asked and what kind of day Clayton had on the water.

They generally left him alone, but tonight's crowd put Clayton ill at ease. Voices already rose to a level beyond conversational: authoritative tones, aggressively assertive, the voices of men and women already deep into a payday Friday evening. He worked his way around one set of voices, a tightly bunched group of three rough-looking men standing mid-bar that he recognized but had never talked with. He was relieved that his customary end stool was available. He felt a bit squeezed but took a seat, pulled his cap over his ears to partially filter the din, and focused on his hands folded on the bar top. Soon, Billy set a mug on the counter and Clayton nodded and sucked at the foam, and then drank more deeply without pleasure.

"What the hell is that?" one of the voices asked, the stockiest of the bunched men.

"What?" one of the others said.

"That fucking smell. Like a rotting corpse."

"How you know what a rotting corpse smell like?"

The man made a show of lifting his nose and sniffing the air and turned to Clayton. "Jesus, man, you ever heard of a bath?"

Clayton did not respond, and did not lift his head to the speaker.

"No wonder your old lady left you, couldn't stand to be in the same house as a stinking dead dick." The man turned to receive the guffaws of his friends just as Clayton's mug struck the back of his head with a dull thud and a spray of beer. He staggered but did not fall, brought a hand to his head, and when it came back bloody, he advanced on Clayton with a smirk. Clayton did not defend himself, did not even rise from the barstool. He saw the man's fist coming square between his eyes and then a halting awareness of Billy's considerable bulk bending over him, his fat, lumpy face scrunched in concern.

"You're OK, right? Here, let me help you up." Clayton tried to reach for Billy's outstretched hand but could not lift his right arm. It refused to work. "Hit your head on the way down," Billy said. "A little stomping went on." Clayton slumped back on the floor.

"Come on, now," Billy said and went behind Clayton, grasped him under the armpits and propped him into a sitting position. Clayton's arm and ribs ached, a shooting pain that brought him to awareness. "Can't have the cops around again. They'll shut me down for sure."

Billy hauled Clayton to his feet, and allowed him a few seconds to steady himself against the bar. "And no ambulance. Bad for business."

Clayton surveyed the room. The boys had left, and the remaining customers sat quietly looking down into their drinks. Billy took him by the elbow, which caused Clayton to flinch, and walked him to the door. "Get on home now. You'll be fine."

Clayton stood at the entrance looking out onto the parking lot, eyes going into and out of focus. His head throbbed in time to the stroboscopic halos pulsing from the streetlights at either end of the lot. He attempted one unsteady step and another.

When Clayton woke on the couch, the light was already streaming through the cottage's east-facing window. His head and his ribs ached, and his left eye would not open beyond a slit. He tested the right arm that had been injured last evening. Merely lifting it from the couch caused a lightning jolt along the length of his arm, and he was unable to flex or straighten his elbow. He rose still wearing his rancid clothes from the day before, went to the porch and with great effort pulled on his overalls and boots. Walking down his drive, he crossed the road and the dunes to the stretch of sand where he kept his beach skiff. The ocean lay calm on a slack tide and he planned to deploy his seine net for the incoming. But, when he tried to drag his skiff from the high tide line down to the shore, pain radiated both down and up from his elbow and his arm became useless. The boat refused to budge. In his younger days, moving the boat had been manageable; but more of a challenge in later years. Dan was just coming of age to be of meaningful assistance when Loretta uprooted him to Ocean City. At fifty-three, Clayton remained capable when all of his parts worked together. But a back spasm or a sprained shoulder could put him out of action. Usually, during tourist season, people hurried to help the eccentric character launching a boat from a crowded beach and setting a fishing net in among the bathers. A story for the neighbors back in Indiana. But the tourist season was over, the beach largely deserted except for a bent-backed shell collector here and there.

Clayton straightened, scowled at the skiff as if it were at fault for refusing to slide itself into the sea, walked back over the dunes and to his johnboat on the marsh side, and spent the afternoon working his crab pots one-armed. Evening, he delivered a sorry catch to the market and collected pay from one of the new owners, a sandy-haired man in his thirties with a welcoming face and engaging manner that reminded Clayton of how Loretta used to interact with the customers.

"Not much to offer today," Clayton said and pointed to his elbow. "Banged up my arm. Slowed me down."

The owner nodded. "Heard there was a little dust-up last night over at Billy's."

Clayton looked toward the door. No keeping things to yourself in a small town. "Too old to be causing a ruckus."

"Well," the owner said, "glad you're not too busted up. Take care of yourself. You still supply the best crab around." He pointed to Clayton's arm. "Ever consider hiring a little help?"

Clayton thought of Dan, closing in on twenty now. Left when he was thirteen, and they'd kept it up: the visits, the summer weeks, for a few years until they just drifted apart. Dan hadn't visited for two years. "Considered it," Clayton said. "But I generally don't get along with people over the long haul."

"Maybe a truck with a winch?"

"Maybe," Clayton said and started for the door. On his way out, he noticed a flyer on the table by the entrance: Giddy Cobb, who ran Giddy's Pet & Play advertising some end-of-season sale. He skimmed the flyer, folded it, and tucked it into his back pocket.

At the cottage, Clayton showered, changed into fresh clothes finally, walked to Billy's, and once again, as was his habit, stood outside debating whether to enter. It was Saturday after all, only marginally less busy than Friday—payday money rolls had shrunk, and the day off provided an opportunity for the drinkers to get their fill already. But the lot was still mostly full. His elbow ached and his vision remained blurred. How had he come to this? Before Loretta left, he'd never been to Billy's; it would never have occurred to him to visit a crowded beer joint. He loved being alone on the water, in his cottage. He loved it to a fault, and it had cost him dearly. Loretta. Dan.

He rested against the side of a pickup in the dimness of the parking lot and weighed his decision against his need to be up and going earlier than usual the following morning—his bad arm would slow him, add time to the baiting, resetting of unproductive traps, harvesting of the crabs. It wasn't beer he craved, necessarily. He regarded enduring the crowded, hectic Billy's as a form of atonement. Penance for the days and weeks he'd enjoyed his solitude at the expense of his relationship with his family.

After a short while, Billy stepped from the bar and approached, baseball bat in hand.

"Who's out there? What the hell you doing?" As he drew near, "That you, Clayton?"

Clayton moved away from the truck. "It is."

Billy held up the bat. "Thought someone was trying to break into the truck."

"Just me," Clayton said.

"Well, you can't stand outside loitering," Billy said, lowering the bat. "Just asking to get clobbered again." He turned toward the bar. "You coming inside?"

"I guess not," Clayton answered, and started home.

Clayton had only recently taken to visiting Billy's. For years following Loretta's departure, he did little but work, eat, sleep, and work. The spit of land she ceded him when she left was his lifeblood—the bay on the marsh side supplied crabs, the oceanside, fish. Those years were a blur of work, sleep, and work.

He took to Billy's only after Dan's visits trailed off. As long as he and Dan maintained a relationship, Clayton felt a part of the family. He'd learn about Loretta and her thriving shop, about Dan's schoolwork and ambitions. When the visits ended, the reality of loss stormed into Clayton's life with gale force. Winter darkness arrived too soon, and summer daylight lingered too long. He could not have expressed even to himself what pulled him to Billy's that first time. Boredom? Curiosity about how others pass time? Clayton's days had never seemed lonely—he'd thrived in his solitude. But after Loretta and Dan moved north, the realization that he no longer had the discretion to choose between company and self-imposed isolation sometimes expressed itself as something akin to loneliness.

That first time Clayton pulled open the door to Billy's, the sights and sounds so assaulted his senses that he left without ever taking a seat. Billy's was neither particularly busy nor rowdy that night, a Tuesday in early August. But the bustle, the pinball machines flashing and pinging, the jukebox blaring, put Clayton on his heels, and he retreated to his cottage, to the racket only of crickets and frogs, so common a sound they barely registered.

Gradually, he acclimated to the disequilibrium, willed himself into Billy's to sit at the end of the bar, to drink his beer, to listen and to observe how others conducted themselves in public, both to their credit and to their shame, to bear his guilt. But, last night unfolded differently. Last night's beating seemed almost a benediction, and he realized he felt the better for it. Redeemed.

Home, Clayton made hot tea, collected his neglected laundry, and sorted it to feed into the tub of the ancient Maytag Wringer. He removed two twenties from the front pocket of his work overalls, payment for the crabs, and retrieved from his back pocket the flyer he'd saved from the market. He unfolded it and read about Giddy Cobb's dilemma. Giddy had arrived in town the summer before and opened Giddy's Pet & Play a petting zoo and playground catering to the children of seasonal tourists looking to give the kids a break from the hot beach and burning sun. "For Sale," the flyer read. "Yearling mule. Harness trained to pull a cart. Asking $400."

"Still learning the business," Giddy explained to Clayton when he stopped by her place the following day. They sat on swing seats in the Pet & Play playground. Giddy swung gently while Clayton uncomfortably anchored his feet on the ground. "Should have known better to have brought a mule into the petting zoo."

"The mule has bad habits?"

"Eddie? No, he's a good mule. Hauls the cart around the ring all day. But doesn't much like being petted by the little tykes. Headbutts, a nip here and there." She pushed off and swung a bit higher.

Clayton rose from the swing, walked to the barn, and stood regarding Eddie. Sturdy, larger than he'd imagined, dark-coated, deep brown, almost black. "How you doing Mr. Ed?" He couldn't bring himself to use the diminutive. The mule's ears flicked.

"Don't know a thing about mules," he said, returning to Giddy.

"Not too much to it. Shelter, food, hoof care. I've closed for the season. I can help out for a while."

"Think he could pull a boat through the sand into the surf?"

Giddy stopped swinging and stood silently for a beat. "Maybe. With a little training."

"I don't have four hundred dollars of a piece."

"I'll take it on time," Giddy said. "I know where you live."

"Well, let me think on it," Clayton said.

"Not too long," Giddy said, looking down the empty October road leading to the summer beach town. "Folks are breaking down the gate to get at this deal."

Clayton built a split-rail pen behind the cottage and outfitted it with a plywood and tar-papered lean-to, and bought galvanized steel feeding and watering troughs. Giddy spent two weeks visiting daily to help acclimate Eddie to his new surroundings and to the harness-and-rope system Clayton rigged to allow the mule to pull his skiff across the sand. Clayton and Giddy got along easily. They understood one another, two small-town eccentrics that stuck out as different—Clayton, an aging lifelong resident of a past time, unattached to the new summer beach crowd, and Giddy, a young newcomer who would depart to parts unknown during the offseason. Would she return the following summer? Who knew?

The mule adapted well. The harness bothered him not at all and he seemed to enjoy the water. Within a week, at the cost of a few carrots, he learned the routine. Giddy led him from the cottage and across a break in the dune line to where the skiff sat at the high tide line. Clayton harnessed him and the mule launched the boat into the surf and would later help pull it back to its resting place.

"I think he's got the hang of it," Clayton said to Giddy. They sat on his porch sipping sweet tea. The afternoon air smelled of wood smoke, and the trees outside the cottage hinted at the season's change. Yellow tinged the edges of leaves, the groundcover showed red. Cool drafts swirled the warm breeze.

"Do you feel confident handling Eddie by yourself?" Giddy asked.

"Do I have a choice?"

She set her glass on the porch. "I need to help on my parents' farm. Pumpkin harvest. Ohio."

"Guess I don't have a choice, then. I'll be all right."

"I'll be back in the spring to kick off tourist season. Memorial Day weekend." She stood.

"I'm guessing it will all be settled between me and Mr. Ed by then. We'll be partners." Clayton rocked gently in his chair and stared into the mid-distance.

"Think I'll just slip on back and say goodbye."

Clayton stood. "Leave me an address and I'll send along my payments."

"Just keep them in a coffee can," Giddy said, looking back from the bottom of the porch. "I'll come collect next spring."

Clayton remained on the porch until Giddy returned from the pen. She waved, and climbed into her truck and eased down the hard-packed lane toward the road into Sand Point. Clayton walked around back, hitched a boot onto the lower pen rail, and studied his mule.

"I don't talk much, Mr. Ed. But I'll treat you fair. I'll let you know what I need from you, and I expect you'll do the same."

The mule's ears twitched and he looked up at Clayton and then back to his water trough. Clayton watched Mr. Ed for a long while, trying to get a sense of his mannerisms, and how he related to this new world, but the mule did not reveal much. He remained in the shelter of the lean-to, tail swishing, looking about now and then, and seeming to regard Clayton as nothing more than another fencepost.

In the days following Giddy's departure, Mr. Ed grew increasingly moody and stubborn. Clayton's injured arm continued to hobble him, perhaps always would—something with the elbow that prevented him from fully extending his arm, that complicated efforts to haul his crab pots or pull his net, let alone launch the boat himself. Without Giddy there to lead him, some days the mule refused to leave the pen no matter how stridently Clayton cajoled or threatened him. Some days Clayton managed to recruit help to launch his skiff, but asking for assistance embarrassed him. With autumn deepening, crabbing slacked off completely, and often when Mr. Ed declined his call to work, Clayton busied himself with putting the garden to bed for the winter and with the constant maintenance required on the boats, nets, and crab pots. But, the blues were running near shore. Stripers too. Clayton needed to be on the ocean. He tried to reason with the mule.

"Here's the deal," he explained, leaning against the rail. "I catch fish. I sell them. You get to eat." He reached into his pocket and retrieved two sugar cubes. "Dessert too."

Mr. Ed lifted his head but did not approach the fence. Clayton held up a bucket of oats. "You don't work, you have no need of grain supplements. Giddy told me."

Mr. Ed brayed.

Clayton set down the bucket. "No fish, no money, no grain. Get it?" He pocketed the sugar cubes. "No treats."

Mr. Ed turned his back to Clayton. Clayton entered the pen and attempted to harness him, but Mr. Ed would have none of it. Finally, Clayton waved a hand in disgust, turned, and walked down the path, across the dirt road, and through the dune line to where his skiff rested. He patted its bow as if it were his favorite pet and looked from it to the surf line some fifty yards distant. "Guess it's not coming to us," he said to the boat. He gathered up the bow harness he'd rigged for Mr. Ed, draped it around his shoulders, and strained toward the water. In the soft sand, his body leaned almost parallel and although his legs bore most of the labor, his elbow ached, shot pain from his forearm to his shoulder where the harness leather bit. He stopped, straightened, took two deep breaths, assessed his progress. A few yards. Where were those tourists when you needed them? He struggled for another few yards and sat on the boat's side rail, massaged his elbow and shoulder, and watched a ghost crab scrabble into its burrow. A shadow appeared in the sand, a sniggering. Mr. Ed lumbered up beside him.

"I guess I left the gate open," Clayton said, standing. He rubbed the mule's ear, offered a sugar cube. "What took you so long?"

Their partnership progressed unevenly during the following months, each taking turns being obstinate, stubborn, thickheaded. But as time passed, they both fell into a routine. Clayton grew to enjoy the mule's company and assumed Mr. Ed felt the same. Giddy Cobb showed up just before Memorial Day weekend as she said she would, and Mr. Ed clearly displayed affection, nuzzling her, and braying. However, when the time came to work, he followed Clayton to the beach without complaint. Walking beside him, Giddy asked Clayton how the winter had gone.

"Long," Clayton said. "Dark." But, with her question came the realization that the time had in fact passed pleasantly enough, that the additional chores involved in having the mule a part of his operation were, in fact, welcome. And, he realized also that he'd not visited Uncle Billy's Bar & Grille since Mr. Ed's arrival.

"But no complaints," he added.

THE ACCIDENT

Loretta called Dan from Ocean City as soon as she arrived home from the emergency room. She had lost her balance on the stepstool while reaching for a box of dishtowels to restock. "The ones with the seashells and that tongue twister," she said. "Fly off the shelf."

"Mom, are you OK?"

"Bound up like a mummy," she said. Two cracked ribs, a separated right shoulder. She asked if he could help out at the boutique, "Just until I can use both arms again and catch a full breath." When Dan did not answer straightaway, she added, "If it's not too much trouble."

It was. It was too much trouble. He did not have the time. Dan's Dependable Used Cars, the dirt lot dealership he'd opened in Sand Point three years earlier was hanging by a fucking thread. The sinkhole of debt threatened to swallow it. Inventory loans meant every vehicle on the lot cost him interest payments each day it sat unsold. He needed to move the metal. He needed to be prowling the lot in Virginia, not pushing dishtowels in Ocean City, Maryland.

AND HE AND ASHLEY had issues to work through. For the past six months, they'd been going back and forth about upping their game, moving in together, even about marriage. But neither seemed compelled to hurry things along. Although Ashley complained about her growing impatience, she always stopped short of issuing ultimatums. Dan lived on the car lot in a trailer that doubled as the sales office, and whenever they discussed setting up house, he clung to that trailer like a life buoy. "Kind of a shady neighborhood. Can't leave the stock unattended."

"Time for the C-word, pal," she told him.

"Co-habitation?" Dan guessed.

"Commitment," Ashley said. Dan sensed a thunderhead building on the horizon.

"YOU SHOULDN'T BE ON A LADDER without someone helping," Dan said to his mother, buying time. Loretta had recently turned sixty-one, a birthday Dan had forgotten, as she'd reminded him. Dan worried about her, about overworking, about the gin and tonics she enjoyed on a nightly basis, about the pills. But he also worried about his business. He'd put so much of himself into it. Everyone had cautioned him not to jump into ownership, to build up to it, to work in a dealership learning the tricks, the ins and outs. He didn't listen. He dove in. The deep end.

"It wasn't a ladder," she said as if that made all the difference. "It was a stool. You know, the little yellow one we keep in the storeroom."

She'd said, "We." Dan realized she still considered them a team, and that one day he'd come to his senses and return to Ocean City and to the boutique. Loretta and he had worked side by side at the shop since she ended her marriage to his father Clayton in 1978. Dan was thirteen when they moved from Sand Point to Ocean City, and even as a teen, Dan controlled boutique stock, managed the part-time summer help, and assisted with the books. When, at age twenty-eight, he finally set out on his own, several times a year Loretta experienced some emergency that required his temporary return: a flood in the basement; the Memorial Day weekend when her assistant quit without notice; the windows that needed boarding in the event the hurricane path shifted.

"I thought you had part-time help," he said.

"Two high school girls who only give me three evenings a week. And a retired guy who still hasn't learned to process credit card purchases. Screws it up every time. I'm going to have to let him go."

"You need his help. Don't fire anyone until I get there." Dan immediately regretted his words.

"Hurry. The summer crowd is showing up. Busy season kicking in."

DAN WALKED FROM THE TRAILER onto the lot. Mid-afternoon, a Wednesday, no action. He had started the dealership with a dozen vehicles: eight cars and four trucks that his father Clayton and Clayton's old friend Sonny Ferrell had helped him condition for sale. Dan knew almost nothing about engine repair or bodywork, just that after years of peddling vacation mementos and seashell ashtrays at the shop, he loved the idea of selling big-ticket items. Clayton had years of experience tinkering and improvising out of necessity, and Sonny was a master auto mechanic. Between them, they put out a reliable and reasonably priced product to get the dealership started.

Now, his inventory totaled between five dozen and six dozen vehicles, half of which he needed to turn over monthly in order to keep his credit line open and to meet his meager payroll. Ashley gave up two days a week at the hair salon and took a cut in salary to help out, and he added a salesman on weekends, oftentimes Sonny, who, although nearing eighty, still moved with vigor, was well known around Sand Point, and took personal offense if someone found fault with an engine he judged fit. His assurances sold a lot of vehicles.

Dan approached Ashley as she strolled among the used vehicles, a dust cloth in hand, wiping the occasional hood. She was an asset to have on the lot. She wore her hair in beach curls that cascaded past her shoulders, and favored slacks and short skirts just "this much" too snug. Sailors from the nearby naval bases would stop by to flirt, and occasionally a sale would result. At times, a tinge of jealousy flared in Dan, and he felt a little cheapened by the marketing tactic. But not often.

They'd met when Ashley came in to buy a used car. She wanted something snappy and fast. After a quick scan of her financial forms, Dan dissuaded her.

"You don't need snappy and fast. You need cheap and dependable."

They went back and forth, Dan arguing her down in price, Ashley insisting up. She laughed, and said that she'd never met a car salesman who tried to downsell.

"Want to role-play?" she asked. "I'll demonstrate how it's supposed to go." She stood, leaned over him, and looked him in the eye. "Dealin' Dan here, and I've got the deal for you." She slapped the desk with her open palm.

Dan countered only half-joking that it would cost more to sell her something over budget only to have to sic the repo men on her.

"Hairy guys. No sense of humor."

They ended going for coffee and talking easily and making one another laugh. Dan marveled at how laughter made his business worries seem almost manageable. Later, when Ashley undressed, Dan thought her to be the most desirable creature he'd ever seen.

Now, after a couple of years together, their ribbing had grown barbed at times. And, he wondered if she might be growing a little wide in the hips. Fleshy? He realized he was no grand prize either—average in every way, average height, average weight, a forgettable face. He and Ashley, a pair. But were they a match? Dan wasn't certain, and neither was Ashley. They debated the issue, and credited themselves for their openness and rationality. Sometimes they took turns voicing the other's strengths and weaknesses. Dan about Ashley: frank, smart, pretty, no, more than pretty; cynical, blunt, condescending at times. Ashley about Dan: outgoing, goal- oriented, attractive, no, more than attractive; glad-handing, obsessed with business success, friendly but impersonal. It was a dangerous game. Usually, they ended up pissed off with each other.

"SAME OLD STORY," Ashley said after Dan explained about Loretta's accident.

"Different story," Dan said. "I don't think she's ever cracked a rib before."

"Attached by a two-hundred-mile umbilical cord."

"It's complicated," Dan said.

"Every family is complicated," Ashley said, and Dan could not argue. Her mother, a family practice attorney, and father, a CPA, threatened to disown Ashley when she declined a college scholarship in favor of cosmetology school. "I love dealing with people," she'd explained to them, "and surveys find that customers trust their hairdressers even more than their bartenders." Needless to add, her parents were further aghast when Ashley announced her relationship with a used car salesman. She and Dan were not often invited to dinner.

Dan had begun wondering recently if Ashley stayed with him only to irritate her parents. He asked himself the same question—why did he remain in a stalled relationship with her? The shallow but honest answer he came up with was sex—never underestimate the bonding power of sex.

"You know you can't afford the time away, right?" Ashley asked.

"I already agreed to go."

"Of course you did."

"I was hoping you and Sonny could cover. I should only be gone a week or so."

"Take a pair of scissors with you," Ashley said, turning away. "Cut that cord."

WHEN DAN ENTERED THE BOUTIQUE, Loretta had her back to him, reaching to rearrange a set of decorative tiles on an upper shelf. Both arms moved freely.

"Mom? What the hell?"

"You must be Dan," the woman said, turning. "I'm your Aunt Kay." She smiled broadly, hands on hips.

Dan stood at the entrance, momentarily speechless. Kay was a younger, fuller version of his mother, like a glimpse into the past. He knew Loretta was the eldest of eleven children, and left home as a teen when several of her siblings were infants. Dan had met a few over the years when one or another showed up on their way from here to there looking for a place to crash or for a loan, "just until the job comes through." But he'd never met Kay, and her resemblance to his mother, except for fuller breasts and an incautious smile, unsettled him.

"There you are." Loretta came from the back of the store. His mother looked worse than Dan had expected—eyes sunken and dull, arm bound tight to her torso, her smile more like a grimace. She'd lost more weight, and her brightly patterned skirt and oversize tunic hung from her in limp folds. "Just in time to drive me home in that fancy car of yours. Need my meds and a short nap."

Loretta insisted Dan keep the top down for the ride. The car was another object of disagreement with Ashley. His birth year car, a 1965 Corvette Sting Ray, soft-top convertible, rally red with black leather interior. Ashley argued he could not have chosen a less practical vehicle to accommodate her and the children they planned to have one day. "One day," Dan had countered. "Not tomorrow, not next week." He'd had the idea to begin stocking his lot with vintage vehicles that would kindle lust in men of a certain age willing, even eager, to pay a premium. The Sting Ray served as a moving advertisement. He'd bet it all on this latest, final marketing scheme to carve his niche in the industry. Although he'd overextended with the finance company, he knew he could close the sales. But not from Ocean City.

"You didn't tell me your sister was here." Dan pulled from the curb, felt his hands clenching the steering wheel.

"Didn't I?" Loretta said.

He turned, glared at her.

"Watch the road," she said.

"So, you don't really need me here."

"I do!" Loretta leaned close and talked loudly over the noise of the engine and the rush of the wind. "I need you to keep an eye on her. I think she's dipping into the cash drawer. And I know she's after my meds. No matter where I hide them, they keep disappearing."

"Have the retired guy watch her," Dan countered.

"Fired him."

"I told you…"

"You were coming. I didn't need him any longer."

They pulled up to the house on the quiet street four blocks inland from the main drag. Dan noticed the postage stamp front lawn in sorry shape. Weeds overtook the strip of garden bordering the sidewalk, and two shrubs on either side of the porch threatened to block the entrance. He resisted the urge to take his mother's free arm to help her up the steps, knowing she would brush his hand away, and together they squeezed between the shrubs and onto the porch. Loretta held out her purse.

"Hold this," she said and fumbled around inside for her keys.

"I can't get over how much your sister resembles you," Dan said. He couldn't bring himself to think of her as "aunt."

"I was better looking at her age," Loretta said. "And slimmer."

"Still," Dan said. "She even dresses like you."

"She dresses like me because she wears my clothes. Showed up here with a suitcase full of crop tops, short-shorts, overalls, and whatnot. At her age?" Loretta retrieved her keys from the bowels of the handbag and worked the lock.

Dan thought perhaps Kay might be able to pull off the look but kept his mouth shut.

"I couldn't have her working in the shop dressed like that," Loretta went on. "Still hasn't found the time or the money to buy her own outfits. Why should she?"

Inside, the rooms were dark, curtains pulled tight, and the stuffy air held the scent of a floral mist he remembered his mother using. And now, likely Kay as well. Dan went to the thermostat, read eighty-one degrees, and fiddled with the lever.

"Doesn't the air conditioning work?"

"I'm always cold these days," Loretta said. "But go ahead."

Dan inched the thermostat setting to seventy-eight and heard the unit kick in, filling the silence with a low hum. "Let me know if you get too uncomfortable," he said and started for his old room. Loretta took the tote bag he carried and tossed it on the sofa.

"Kay took my clothes, took your room."

The sofa was fine with Dan, a visible reminder to his mother that the visit was temporary. And, the bedroom he'd lived in from age thirteen to twenty-eight held little nostalgia. The house itself never had seemed like home. Nor had Ocean City. The gaudy lights, the boardwalk Elvis cruising in his white v-neck jumpsuit with the puff sleeves and artificial crotch bulge, the cheesy haunted house, the mini-golf extravaganzas, and Bozo the clown at the dunking pool, hurling insults at passersby. The ocean seemed almost an afterthought. It set Dan on edge, so different from Sand Point with the wide, empty stretches of sand, the rolling dunes, the insistent mewing of the gulls, and the slapping waves. In truth, he loved being with his father in Sand Point but tired of the seclusion after a few days. He loved being with his mother in Ocean City but shied from the bustle after a few days. With the shuffling back and forth, he'd never fully settled in either place.

Loretta went to the sofa, reached beneath the center cushion, and retrieved a medicine bottle. She poured the contents into her palm, counted, and returned the pills, less two that she popped into her mouth and chewed dry. "She hasn't found them yet."

"Careful there," Dan said.

Loretta pointed to her shoulder and walked toward her room. "If you don't mind, can you check on Kay? See that she hasn't cleaned us out?"

AFTER ONLY A DAY in the boutique, it became clear to Dan he was not needed, and he chafed at being away from Dan's Dependable Used Cars. Although Kay was an open flirt, possibly on the hunt for a new husband, she did help around the store, and she harbored no malicious intent toward Loretta, indeed held her in high regard.

"Did you know that your mother sent money to us every month until all of us kids were done with our schooling?"

"I didn't," Dan admitted.

"Kept us out of the poorhouse."

Also, Kay had not been sneaking Loretta's pills. "They are disappearing down her throat," she told Dan. "Haven't you noticed how loopy she is?"

"She's in a lot of pain," Dan said. Kay started to say something, but instead just pursed her lips.

It was his mother's condition rather than the boutique that kept Dan in Ocean City for an extra two days. He had worried about Loretta's habit for over a decade. He knew that as a young woman, a girl really, she'd been married to a much older, abusive son-of-a-bitch, and when he died she became driven to make a success of the small grocery she'd inherited. When Clayton came along, he was of some help, but his reclusiveness ill-suited him to retail life. Loretta began with the pills to pep her up during the day and to allow sleep at night, a routine Dan knew she'd continued through the years. Recently, the cumulative impact of her abuse seemed to have caught up with her, and Dan needed to monitor her, to assess permanent damage. He could watch her for a day or two, perhaps plan how to get her help, and still be back in Sand Point by the weekend.

The evening of the second day of his stay, the three of them drank gin and tonics on the back deck after work, watching the billowed clouds turn orange with the last of the sun.

"I'm hitting the boardwalk," Kay announced. "Want to come?"

"I'm having another drink," Loretta said.

"I have some calls to make," Dan said. Perhaps with Kay out of the house, he could gently confront his mother, suggest a substance abuse program he'd found in the yellow pages.

"We live in a beach resort, for heaven's sake." Kay went to her room and returned a few minutes later in a yellow, fish-print sundress with spaghetti straps and a deep V-neck.

Loretta eyed the outfit. "That's not mine."

"Bought it today," Kay said. "Like it?"

"Prowling?" Loretta asked.

"Don't wait up," Kay answered.

Kay left and Loretta went to the kitchen for another gin and tonic. Dan heard the phone ring. Loretta answered and called to him. "It's Ashley."

In the kitchen, Dan took the receiver from Loretta. "I was going to call you this evening."

"You know the '68 Charger?" Ashley asked.

"Bronze with the black accent stripes?"

"That's the one."

"Great muscle car. One of the early models."

"Well," Ashley said, "it's gone."

"Sold?" Dan allowed himself a surge of excitement. "Great work, hon."

"No," Ashley said. "Gone."

"Gone?" Deflated, he began pacing the kitchen, the phone cord stretching and slacking. "What the fuck does that mean?"

"Guy comes in for a test drive. Doesn't come back."

Dan began mentally running the calculations—the insurance deductible, the increase in premiums, the temporary tag replacement. "You got his driver's license info, right?" He knew the answer but asked anyway.

"Stolen."

"Jesus, Ashley. I asked you to watch the place for a few days, and this."

"It's my fault? I knew it. Some jerk drives away with your car, and you blame me."

"Whose fault would it be?"

"Let me think," she says, and waits, one beat, two. "Oh, you're the one who left to take care of Mommy."

Dan, in his thinking afterward, showed otherworldly restraint. "Call the police. I'll talk to the insurance company."

"I'm doing OK," Ashley said. "Thanks for asking."

"It's not like he had a gun," Dan said. "I have to go."

"By the way," she said. "I'm late."

"Late for what?" In the pause that followed, Dan slowly pieced it together.

"Wait. Late? What about the pill? This was never in the plan. Damn it all. I have no time for this."

The response to Dan's outburst was a prolonged silence followed by Ashley's calm, resigned, voice. "Don't worry, I'll take care of things one way or the other. Goodbye, Dan."

"We'll talk tomorrow when I get home," Dan said.

"No. You don't understand. Goodbye."

Dan continued pacing as the dial tone transitioned to the sharp staccato of the off-hook signal. He held the receiver at arm's length and stared at it dumbly as if waiting for a more complete explanation of what just happened, the layered complications of his life testing his ability to make sense of it, to cope. Finally, he hung the handset on the wall mount and made another gin he had not intended, and joined Loretta on the deck. The confrontation with his mother could wait. He had other worries.

SOMETIME DEEP INTO THE NIGHT, Dan woke on the sofa to the sound of a key working the door lock and sensed Kay come through the living room and pause beside the sofa. Dan feigned sleep. After a few moments, she turned and walked toward the bathroom, trailing a scent of cigarettes and sweet citrus. Dan listened to the toilet flushing and the water running. When the door opened, Kay stood in her bra and panties, leaning against the doorframe, backlit by soft light, watching him. Dan remained motionless, eyes a slit, horrified by the creepiness of the scene, but unable, unwilling, to turn away. Kay stepped from the doorway and flicked off the light. Dan sensed her there still, in the dark, waiting. Finally, she moved into the bedroom and eased the door shut. Dan shifted onto his back and stared up at nothing, trying to erase the images, trying to tamp down his imagination. He needed away from this place.

Kay slept late the following morning, but Loretta rose early looking like she'd hardly rested. Her eyes were bagged and her complexion pallid. Dan poured them both coffees.

"Eggs?"

"Just toast," Loretta said. "Maybe some strawberry jam."

Dan made the toast and they sat at the small cafe table off the kitchen.

"I'm going home tonight," he said. "After we close shop."

Loretta straightened. "You just got here."

"You and Kay have things under control. I need to get back to the lot."

"Wait," Loretta stood. "I have a surprise for you. I've been saving it, didn't know you'd be in such a rush." She went to her bedroom and returned with a folder and set it in front of him.

"Mom, what's this?"

"I know you've been struggling. I have the answer."

Dan flipped open the folder and scanned the legal documents. Transfer of ownership, Loretta's Boutique, lacking only his signature.

"I figure you can keep me on staff," Loretta said. She leaned toward him, a beseeching smile. Words came to Dan's mind but he held them there, unspoken. *Pathetic. Desperate. Unbalanced.* During his silence, Loretta's smile froze, and her eyes shot back and forth between the papers on the table and Dan's face.

"Mother, I'm staying in Sand Point." He watched as she wilted, and fought the urge to comfort her. "I am not coming back. You need to accept that." He closed the folder and pushed it away.

They barely conversed at the boutique. Dan worked the floor while Loretta spent most of the day behind the checkout counter. On the few occasions they encountered one another, they both looked away and passed without acknowledgment. Kay reported late, appearing a bit pale but otherwise buoyant. Around four, Dan left to ready for the drive home—gas up, grab some snacks, and pack. At eight, Kay arrived at the house, showered, and dressed for another evening out. Dan wondered if she might bring up last night, but she only hinted.

"I shouldn't be too late. If you're awake we can visit."

"Is Mom still at the shop?"

"Did you two have an argument?"

"Not exactly."

"Said she'd be along soon," Kay said. As she passed Dan on her way to the door, she rested her hand on his lower back. "Later," she said.

Dan decided to delay leaving until he could say goodbye to his mother, smooth things over a bit.

He never got the chance.

The two officers stopped by at nine, or a bit past the hour. Dan did not know them, but they were acquainted with Loretta, a fixture in town. A nice lady, they said. We liked her. The car had wrapped around a tree after crossing the lane at high speed, jumping the ditch, and rolling twice. She wasn't found in the car. After going through the windshield, she ended up sitting against a white picket fence, as if at rest. Except for the blood and the missing parts. The officers only implied the missing parts, when explaining that it was not necessary for Dan to identify the body. No, they said. Do not view her.

After the officers left, Dan sat on the sofa awhile. His thoughts darted, drifted. His mother would arrive soon. They'd make drinks, sit on the deck, and view the neon glow from the boardwalk. He rose from the sofa, walked to the kitchen, made a gin and tonic for himself and one for his mother, set them on the table, walked outside, looked over the neighborhood, the lights from living rooms and the stroboscopic flashing from TVs, smelled the ocean four blocks over, imagined the sea rolling in like it did every day after day after day, from the time Loretta came into this world until she left it, and would continue rolling in from the time Dan came into this world until he left it. Lives passed, the sea remained, and Dan knew it fell to him to tell his father. He was of the sea, his father, and would turn away from Dan; Dan knew this. In his mourning, Clayton would meld deeper into the sand and the water, the only place he might find solace.

Dan had spent his life trying to fit into both his mother's world and his father's. Now he would have neither, and that thought intertwined with his grief and magnified it. He wished he had answers, something to make sense, how to fit into his own world, and he suddenly wished to have someone there on the sofa beside him to talk things out, and then he realized he'd soon have Kay on the sofa, that he would have to look into the face of a younger Loretta and tell her his mother, her sister, was dead, and how would Kay take the news, would she come to him for comfort and how would he respond? He left before Kay returned.

DAN NAVIGATED THE TWO-LANE blacktop leading to Sand Point in the hour before dawn. He drove incautiously, powering through curves, accelerating on the straights. The maneuvers were a distraction. He was in no hurry. Although his father and mother had not spoken much in the past decade, Dan knew that Clayton had never left Loretta, that she remained a part of him, and that the news Dan carried would shift Clayton's world, and honestly, Dan wished he did not have to be the one to deliver it. But Clayton hardly ever answered his phone, failed to the several times Dan tried over the past several hours, and it seemed cruel and unfeeling to leave a recorded message or to rouse Sonny Ferrell to convey the news.

On his way into town, impulsively he detoured to Dan's Dependable Used Cars, idled in front of the locked gate, and surveyed his lot. The vehicles lurked in the darkness, metal hulks, animalistic, crouched. His. This was his family. These were his children. Something suddenly became clear to him, something decided. He shifted into first and continued on.

Nearing Sand Point, thick stands of loblolly pine and bald cypress lined either side of the road, and dense underbrush created the sensation of driving through a lightless tunnel. Here and there the view opened onto fields of corn and potatoes just visible in the dim light. Where creeks and inlets approached the road, a spectral fog hung in low pockets, forcing Dan to steer by instinct. Along one such stretch, the shortened reach of his headlamps suddenly illuminated two bright dots low to the ground, and a pop sounded from under his tires. A raccoon? Opossum? Cat? Dan continued without stopping.

Cautious now, he imagined how easily one might become disoriented, distracted by the weather or by unwelcome thoughts, miss a curve, drift, end up in a ditch, or around a tree.

Was it his fault? His mother? His relationship with Ashley? Both wrecked.

Turning onto the winding, unpaved drive leading to his father's shack among the scrawny pine and twisted tupelo between the second dune line and the beginning of the salt marsh, Dan worried that his Corvette might not have the clearance. Twice the undercarriage thumped against the uneven hard pack or a jutting root, but slowly he crawled it into the clearing and parked beside Clayton's pickup. He sat behind the wheel, unable for the moment to move. For all that had occurred in the past twelve hours, for all that he knew needed to be done, he'd not actually planned how he might break the news. He considered for a moment turning around to collect Sonny Ferrell, a buffer between Dan and his father. The door of the screened porch opened, and Clayton appeared. He squinted into the glare of the headlamps. Dan cut the engine and opened the door and willed himself from the Sting Ray.

THE LAST DUNE

Clayton Royster began constructing his modest cottage in 1966, on an inaccessible thumb of land that jutted between the sea and the saltmarsh inlet near the town of Sand Point, Virginia. Cinderblock-by-cinderblock, scrap-by-scrap, he tucked it into a stand of sweetgum and wax myrtle on high ground behind the second dune line. Over the years, he added piecemeal improvements: indoor plumbing, a screened porch, electricity, and a slapdash workshop. Against current city code, he kept a boat on the beach above the high tide mark and, also against code, a black mule in a pen at the far side of his property, where the salt marsh began reclaiming habitable ground. He filled his days fishing and crabbing both for his table and to supply the roadside markets, setting a gill net for baitfish when he needed folding money, and tending his garden.

He'd built the cottage originally as a refuge when the urge for solitude pulled him from family, and settled there permanently after Loretta and he split and she left. Now, its age-weary exterior was so woven with Virginia creeper that it appeared as something extruded from the earth, and it reflected tepid inhospitality Clayton neither intended nor disavowed.

Alone and content among the dunes and the overgrown brush, the years scrolled. The twice-monthly visits with his son Dan gradually tapered. The seasons on the water followed a predictable rhythm: fifteen-hour days during summer spent fishing, crabbing, netting, and gardening; less hectic winter months with time to catch up on rest and repairs, both to body and equipment. Over the years, brief moments of existential crisis punctuated the routine—the appendicitis that almost killed him before he surrendered to the pain and made his way to the clinic, the outboard motor that hit a submerged log, bucked, and lurched him wearing full winter gear into the surf. Emergencies aside, Clayton lived a simple life, until it became complicated.

In 2010, the city claimed through eminent domain a strip of his land to extend the beach road and to construct a bridge over the inlet, uniting the communities on either side. By 2012, after almost five decades of isolation, his property became accessible. Traffic oftentimes drowned out the sound of the sea and the whoop and chirr of night creatures. All who drove along the new road marveled at the undeveloped oceanfront, the last stretch of open beach for miles in either direction. Some coveted.

CLAYTON SAT ON A LAWN CHAIR inside the screened porch waiting out the heat of midday, whittling a large stick into a small stick. He watched the man come up the path, stumbling over vines that crisscrossed it like tripwires. The man stepped cautiously around Clayton's derelict truck as if it might lurch at him given the slightest provocation. He raised his cell phone to eye level, slowly turned in a circle, stopped facing the cottage, and lowered his phone. "Mr. Royster?" he called.

Clayton rose, folded, and pocketed his jackknife, dusted shavings from his pants, and stepped from the porch into the fog of scents that mingled in the still air of the clearing: damp loam, lowland decay, ripening manure. Heat and a soft light sifted through the thin canopy of leaves. "I am Clayton."

"I'm Jason. Left a business card in your mailbox?"

With his unnatural shock of white-blond hair and equally unnatural penny-colored tan, Jason seemed better suited to flip-flops and bathing trunks than to the casual business attire he wore. His short-sleeved blue cotton shirt showed dampness at the collar. Clayton couldn't help but picture him on one or another of those wave-riding contraptions that got in the way of his netting operation. It put him off the boy, even before hearing him out.

"I liked the other one better. Prettier."

"Jennifer?" Jason asked.

"Your wife?"

"My boss."

"How is that, working for a lady?"

"Great. It's great." Jason launched into the pitch, a minor variation of what Clayton heard from Jennifer a few days before, except that Jason sweetened the offer.

"You taking telephone pictures of my place?" Clayton asked.

Jason held up his phone. "In case you decide to list with us. Need photos. OK?"

"No. No, it is not OK."

"Of course. Should have asked first." Jason slid the phone into his back pocket. "So, our offer?"

Clayton glanced around the salvage heap of his lot, a hallelujah of chaos: rusted propellers, an engine block, six cardboard refrigerator boxes broken down and stacked against the side wall, PVC pipe in various lengths scattered about like pickup sticks. "Can't imagine who would want to pay that kind of money for this."

"Well," Jason began hesitantly, "and the beach lots, of course."

"Beach lots," Clayton mulled, as if the realization had sunk in just that instant, his three hundred feet of oceanfront. "We best take a look."

They walked the path toward the road. Although sweat streaked the back of Jason's shirt, Clayton was comfortable in his four-season outfit, denim trousers and a chambray work shirt, worn thin from washing and soft as fine linen. At the road, they stood looking over the expanse of sand leading to the line of dunes that rose like ocean swells to obscure the water view. An offshore breeze fluttered tuffs of sea oats dotting the sand and delivered the sound of surf breaking and the smell of brine and seaweed. Within Clayton's memory, the entire shoreline stretched like this for miles in either direction. But over time the dunes had been leveled to ease construction, or remolded into mild perches for the luxury homes. The dunes were gone now, except for his, and he cherished them like the last survivors of an extinct species.

"Build here?" Clayton asked.

"Yes."

"Like those other places?" He turned, pointed. The side of his face and outstretched hand were the brown, leathered carapace of a horseshoe crab, but the back of his neck where his shirt collar pulled away showed white as bleached oyster shells.

"Sure, maybe. But upscale. Modern."

"And my place? What's to become of it?"

Jason frowned in concentration and narrowed his eyes. "What would you like to see happen with it? I'm sure we could take your wishes into consideration."

"I'm sure," Clayton smiled thinly. "Best get back to work. Thanks for stopping by." He turned and started across the road, his movement even-gaited on the sand but becoming tentative, almost wary, when crossing the asphalt scar. Once across, his pace picked up and he crested the far dune with an ancient grace, and disappeared into the scrub thicket.

MID-MORNING, JUNE WINDING DOWN, Clayton stood beside his boat, ran his hand along the gunwale, and looked out over the water.

"What do you think, Mr. Ed? Should we take her out?"

For years they had fished together, the mule and he. Harnessed with a homespun breast collar and a rope tied to the prow cleat, Mr. Ed would haul the skiff into the surf for the price of a sugar cube, wait while Clayton set the net, and for a second cube return the boat to its resting place beyond the high water mark. The mule was worked out now, as was Clayton, although at times when the tides ran strong and the fish schooled, something in Clayton's DNA, some muscle memory, drew him to his boat. Watching the gulls shriek and dive into water oil-slicked with baitfish, time blended, then into now, now into then, the seasons of a man braided, and Clayton decided, yes, we should fish.

There came a tap on his shoulder. Another more firm. Clayton turned.

"Junior. I didn't notice you come up on me."

Crew-cut, tending toward husky, with biceps the size of small buoys, Junior sat astride his city-issued ATV not two feet from Clayton. He wore a short-sleeved khaki shirt emblazoned with "Beach Safety & Animal Control" insignias. "Hard to sneak up on a man with this thing." Junior goosed the throttle.

"Guess I did probably hear you coming," Clayton said. "But didn't give it any notice. Thinking about setting my net."

Junior glanced at the boat. Sand drifted halfway up a sun-faded blue lapstreak hull badly in need of caulking. Behind the aft bench, a cracked rubber hose tethered a rust-flecked red gas tank to an ancient outboard motor not worth the stealing. "Don't think this rig is going anywhere anytime soon," he said. "Take a backhoe to dig it out."

Junior dismounted the ATV and rapped his knuckles on the bow deck. "Which reminds me. Remember that notice to remove it from the public beach?"

"I own this stretch of beach," Clayton answered.

"Not seaward of the dune. Public beach, public access. You know that."

"I've kept this boat here for more years than you've been walking this earth."

"Doesn't make it legal. A nuisance. Injury hazard. And, don't even think about setting your net with all these people about."

Indeed, since the road was extended, bathers had begun appearing on his once sparsely visited stretch of sand, spreading blankets, anchoring umbrellas, staking claim.

"Got to set the net when the fish are running," Clayton said, patiently.

"That tourist from New Jersey?" Junior said, referring to few summers ago, when Clayton could still on occasion manage the netting operation.

"What kind of fool swims hisself into a net?"

"I don't think he knew it was a net."

"Guess he knows one now."

Mr. Ed brayed and dropped a load of manure onto the sand beside the boat.

"And him," Junior added, pulling a citation pad from his back pocket.

FOLLOWING THE JULY HOLIDAY, code enforcement warnings began arriving in the mail, irritating to Clayton as the black flies that buzzed in his ear when he cleaned Mr. Ed's stall. First warning, swatted away, second warning, swatted. The final warning gave him two weeks to clean his property of overgrown weeds, refuse, and hazardous materials before the city would send a crew and charge him for the work. He let them accumulate with Mr. Ed's unpaid citations on his nightstand until the tax delinquency notice moved him to action. His truck refused to turn over, and rather than take the time to repair it, he rode Mr. Ed bareback into town, causing traffic to back up and a line of tourists to line the sidewalk in gawking delight. He hitched Mr. Ed to a parking meter in front of the courthouse, went inside, and wandered the halls until he stumbled upon the county clerk's office.

"What is this about?" Clayton tossed the code warnings onto the desk and pointed at them accusingly. An affable if unsmiling woman of indeterminate age, they all looked young to Clayton, collected the papers, asked for a moment, returned, and fanned out several pictures depicting his yard in various stages of disarray.

"These are code violations," she said.

"Never had one show up before."

"Well, city codes do change, are updated to the times." She tapped the folder. "Received several complaints."

"From who?"

"We're not at liberty," she started, but Clayton waved her off.

"And this?" he offered the tax bill.

The woman glanced at it briefly. "That is a notice of delinquency. Your tax is overdue."

"It's off. Almost double last year. I called you about it."

The clerk again asked for a moment and returned with another folder. "Yes, I see that you did. We explained that you were free to file a formal protest. Remember?"

He did not. Or, maybe he remembered bits of the conversation, but not whether he followed up.

"Well, then, I protest."

"It's too late. The deadline for the current tax year is past."

"But it's wrong. The tax is not right."

She took the invoice from him and examined it closely and slid it back to him almost tenderly. "I don't think a protest would have changed anything. The bill is based on the current assessment of your property value using comparable houses in the neighborhood."

"Neighborhood? I don't live in any neighborhood." As the clerk's tone softened, Clayton's frustration multiplied.

"There's lots of new construction out your way." She handed him back his tax notice. "With the new road and all."

Outside, Clayton found Junior at the curb, writing on his pad, and below Mr. Ed, a pile of mule shit pungent on the hot asphalt.

"Another ticket?" Clayton asked.

"I'm just getting started," Junior said, pointing with his pen to the car occupying the parking space next to them. The front headlight lens lay in pieces on the sidewalk and the lamp dangled from its connector socket. A man in a white polo and pink slacks paced back and forth in front of the car, his jaw worrying the stub of a cigar, his scowl alternating between his grille, Mr. Ed, and Clayton.

"Must've spooked him," Clayton said. "Just a mule being a mule."

"That animal belongs in a glue gun," the man said and flung his cigar to the sidewalk. Clayton moved around Junior, stubbed the butt with his heel, and dropped it into a green trash receptacle. "Shouldn't ought to litter." The man sputtered, and took a step toward Clayton, but stopped short when Junior stepped between them. The man removed his cell phone from his back pocket and retreated into the courthouse.

"Don't know how you can afford to keep Mr. Ed," Junior said.

"I can manage just as long as I don't pay the fines."

Junior handed Clayton the two new citations. "For your collection."

Clayton untied Mr. Ed and began to lead him away, but Junior paused him with a hand on his shoulder. "Seriously, Mr. Royster. One too many complaints and we're going to have to confiscate him."

"Mr. Ed's been with me a long while."

"Town's growing," Junior said. "Getting crowded. The mule doesn't belong here anymore. His time is past."

CLAYTON COULDN'T REMEMBER exactly how old Mr. Ed was, but he had to be going on thirty, maybe more. It was after Loretta left him. Or, he left her. Or, they'd finally given up on one another, something he never saw happening until it did. Dan was just coming of age to help with the fishing operations when Loretta left with him. Clayton, needing help, decided he'd prefer spending his days working with a four-legged assistant than a two-legged one who would require civil interaction and occasional conversation.

He came by the mule from Giddy Cobb. She owned Giddy's Pet & Play, located a few miles from the beach on the main road into Sand Point. Giddy came and went with the seasons, showing up with her menagerie in mid-May, and departing in September after Labor Day. But not all of her animals left with her. Several each season had to be moved from the petting zoo to a more appropriate habitat—a farmers' fattening lot for example, or to the goat cheese operation inland.

Giddy and Clayton were acquainted, visited occasionally, attracted to one another, perhaps, because they shared the distinction of being judged social outliers. When it became known that Clayton was in the market for a work animal, and when one of Giddy's mules in its transition from infancy to adolescence had taken to nipping the hands that reached to pet him and bucking the fannies that sought to sit him, the transaction seemed preordained.

Clayton knew that Mr. Ed could not live forever, but he had in recent years come to hope that he, Clayton, might go first, sparing him both the pain of loss and the bother of disposal.

CLAYTON AWOKE DURING the second hour of a new day and felt the tidal pull in his blood. He rose and dressed without turning on a light, allowing his eyes to adjust. He transferred three menhaden and belly meat from a small dogfish from a bag in the refrigerator to his orange five-gallon bucket and tossed a water bottle in as well. After downing half a cup of yesterday's coffee poured cold from the percolator, he went outside, harnessed Mr. Ed, and fitted him with a canvas pannier to which he lashed his fishing gear, the ancient Penn level-wind, and the fiberglass rod, along with several scraps of cardboard, PVC pipe, and tarpaper from his yard's stockpile.

Along the beach, a lopsided August moon lit his way and cast diamonds on the quiet water. He wondered if others might already be camped by the slough he wished to fish, but when he arrived, he saw no one. He set to work on his fishing shack, a lean-to built from PVC pipes he anchored in the sand and layered first with cardboard and then with tarpaper in the event weather blew in with daylight. Weary from the effort, he tethered Mr. Ed to one of the anchor pipes, tied a feedbag around his head, and stooped inside his hut to rest until the slack tide began to run.

He overslept, awakened late to a full sun bearing down. Where was he, and why? The stench of menhaden ripening in the rising heat jogged his memory, and he began preparing his bait, cutting strips from the fish and tossing heads, innards, and bones back into the bucket to be used in his crab pots. As he reached for the last of the menhaden, a shadow crossed the opening of the shack and he glanced up to find a young girl of perhaps five looking in on him.

"Hello there," Clayton said. One hand held the skeleton of the fish with only the head attached and the gut sack dangling. In the other hand, a bloody filet knife. The girl ran screaming. For a moment, Clayton wondered if he might be imagining things. What would a little girl be doing this far down the beach? Someone should be watching after her.

He cleaned his hands on a rag, crawled from the shack, took up his rod, threaded a strip of bait onto his hook, waded into the surf until thigh-deep, and cast into the slough between the shore break and the near sandbar. He reeled the slack in his line until he felt his sinker bouncing along the bottom with the current. Nothing to do now but wait for the fish.

A whistle sounded, loud and shrill. Clayton turned, saw Junior standing beside his ATV, and raised a hand to him. He turned back to his fishing.

Again, the whistle. "Come on in here," Junior called. "I am in no mood to get wet this early."

Clayton released line from the reel spool, backed onto the sand, set the tension, and fitted the butt of the rod into a holder sunk into the sand. A few strands of seaweed dangled from the line that ran glistening from the tip of his rod into the water forty yards out.

"What are you doing, Clayton?"

"Trying to catch supper." He watched the rod tip for movement. "A flounder, maybe a blue."

"I mean, what are you up to with that litter on the beach?"

"My fishing shack."

"That what you call it?"

"Been putting one up around here for years."

"Not allowed. City code."

"Not allowed? Out here in the middle of nowhere?"

"Clayton, you are not making any sense."

Clayton turned to face Junior, started to argue, and then his expression went slack. Behind Junior, behind Clayton's tarpaper lean-to, behind Mr. Ed, loomed a four-story hotel a block long. When had this happened? With its Caribbean blue lap-siding and peach trim, it looked as out-of-place to Clayton as he realized Mr. Ed must have seemed to the tourists studying the mule from their balconies. Unable to process the monstrosity, the desecration of his life-land, Clayton looked away. People in tight scrums stood at a cautious distance watching. They blurred in and out of focus, dabs of color only, elongated shapes against a flat backdrop. He smelled Mr. Ed beside him and concentrated on that reality, the odor of leather and canvas, the sweat and dust from the pen, and the sea salt caked on his hide, and that calmed him. Junior hovered near, his broad face scrunched in puzzlement. "The father said you were butchering something in there."

Clayton tried to make sense of it all. This was his fishing spot, had been forever.

"Junior, I was cutting bait."

"The father thought your hut was some kind of public art installation, sent his little girl to check it out. Scared her to death."

"Cutting bait."

"And, some of those folks," Junior said, gesturing with his thumb, "are still wondering if you might not be one of those living history exhibits." He chuckled, not unkindly. "Let me help you get this stuff packed up."

Gear stowed, Clayton took Mr. Ed's halter and turned for home.

"You need anything else?" Junior asked. "You'll be OK?"

"I'm set." Clayton started down the beach, but something caught his attention and he paused, looking upward. An osprey hovered above the surf break as if suspended by some celestial thread. For seconds it held stationary in the air current before folding its wings, diving, and exploding into the water. A moment later it surfaced, rose with empty talons, shook water from its feathers as it climbed into the sky, and resumed hunting.

"Five, six times in a row," Clayton said. "Five, six times it will come up empty."

"That's persistence," Junior offered.

"That's life," Clayton said and continued down the beach.

"Clayton," Junior stopped him. "Have you thought about talking to a lawyer?"

Clayton turned. "For what? Am I in trouble with the law?"

"No. That's not my point."

"Then why would I need a lawyer? A few unpaid tickets?"

"More than a few. But it's not the citations."

"Then what?"

"I've no business discussing this." Junior searched the sky for the osprey. "There's talk around the APS."

"The what?"

"Adult Protective Services."

"And just what is this APS talking about?"

"Some think you'd be better off with someone watching you."

"Watching me do what?"

Junior ran a hand through his short hair and wiped perspiration on his pant leg. "Clayton, you are making this hard."

"Don't mean to. Just can't imagine who would be interested in watching me go about my business."

CLAYTON SCRUBBED THE CORROSION off the battery posts and cable ends with a wire brush and the truck started with only mild protest. He avoided the four-lane thoroughfares as best he could before easing onto the interstate for an uncomfortable six miles until he came to the billboard with the image of Dan pointing the way to the exit. A thirty-foot American flag signaled the entrance to the dealership. It had been a few years since Clayton last visited, just before the work on the new showroom began, and the operation had grown substantially from what he recalled. Gone was the two-bay garage where he'd helped Dan recondition the first dozen or so cars he'd put on the lot almost twenty years earlier.

Inside the showroom, sales cubicles rimmed a circular open space displaying used cars and trucks: a jeep in full camouflage, a black Mercedes sedan, and a metallic blue Camaro from the seventies. Two flat screens the size of garage doors hung from the ceiling back-to-back, and both featured Dan, giving his latest sales pitch. "Hey buddy," the voice boomed from surround-sound speakers, "Here at Dependable Used Cars I'll find you the perfect vehicle to suit your budget and your needs. I'm Dan, and that's my promise to you. Each time. Every time." Clayton watched, mesmerized. He could not fit the voice to his son's face. Dan he recognized, of course, an older version of the boy, if gone a little pudgy, the softness that some wealthy men seem to develop. But the voice, the shouting from the screen in frenetic enthusiasm, was completely foreign.

He turned from the monitor, went to the reception desk, and asked to speak with Dan. The receptionist looked up from her computer with a practiced smile, freezing only for a moment at the sight of an old man wearing faded Carhartt jeans and a flannel work shirt. "Absolutely!" she beamed. "Dependable Dan visits the floor every day between five and six. Right out front here. He loves to meet his customers."

"Dan and I are acquainted. Is he in?"

"Sorry. Meetings. All day." She held her smile.

"I'll wait over there," Clayton pointed to a chair. "Tell him his father needs a word."

The receptionist hesitated, perhaps calibrating her internal security radar, swiveled in her chair, crunched over, and talked quietly into her headset. Shortly, Dan emerged from the one office with solid walls that guarded it from view. "Dad, what the heck? Come on in."

Clayton stood and followed Dan. "Quite a flag you have out there."

"Fifteen grand of patriotism on display," Dan said. His voice boomed, like in the commercial, but once into the office with the door shut, it dropped in range and volume, from showboat salesman to just Dan. "Dad, what's up?" He motioned, and they sat.

"What do you know about this APS business?" Clayton asked.

Dan did not show surprise at the question. "We talked two months ago, remember? About part-time help? Again last month."

"Help with what?"

"The medicines you keep forgetting to take. The meals you skip, a little cleaning, maybe."

"I do remember that talk."

"Good," Dan said.

"I remember saying no," Clayton said.

Dan slumped in his chair. "Dad, listen to me. Just because you refuse help doesn't mean you don't need it."

"Is this where this Adult Protective Services comes in?"

"I've talked to them, just to get some information, learn our options."

"Options?"

"Day nurse, home healthcare, maybe a retirement community, someplace nice, where you can keep active."

"I keep plenty active as it is. In fact, I have to get to work." Clayton started to rise, but Dan motioned him back into his chair.

"Listen to me, Dad. APS is the least of it. They told me about bloodsuckers out there, private companies that petition the courts for guardianship. Take you against your will, stick you in some dump, sell your property to cover expenses. I want us to act before they do."

"So, you want to be first to put me away?"

"What do I know about this business? I'm trying to figure it all out, but I don't have a clue. I'm losing sleep."

"No need to. Just let things alone."

Dan straightened and slapped his thigh. "Fine. Picture this. You fall, have a stroke, heart attack, whatever. Spend two days wallowing in your own waste before anyone thinks to check on you. How does that sound?"

"Sounds better than having some young girl wipe my backside for me."

"Listen to reason for once."

"What does your mother have to say about your plan?"

Dan leaned close. "What?"

"Your mother. What does Loretta think?"

Dan stared at Clayton for a full ten seconds without speaking, and then, softly, "Oh, Dad."

Clayton's eyes went blank for a moment, unfocused, and then returned. He waved his hand dismissively. "Never mind." He rose and walked to the door. Dan followed him to the truck.

"Still driving this thing," Dan commented, as Clayton climbed behind the wheel. "One of the first vehicles I ever sold. You bought it."

Clayton cranked the engine. "Not running like it should. A lemon, maybe." He eased away.

"Think about things," Dan called. "I'll stop by in a couple days."

STORMS ARRIVED WITH A VENGEANCE that September. During the night, lightning flashed, illuminating the room for an instant and then plunging it back into darkness. On, off. On, off. Clayton woke, slept, and dreamt of running his johnboat out into the sound on summer mornings, setting his crab traps, the Jimmies that brought top dollar. Sleep, flashes, Loretta beside him, nesting and content. Flashes, his restless pacing at night, his need for solitude, that time he burrowed into a dune while lightning pierced the sky, the rain pelting. Another flashing, and he woke fully, rubbed awareness into his eyes, rose, paced his cottage, the coffee pot here, his boots beside the door. He went outside, forgetting the boots. Out back, Mr. Ed huddled under the protection of his pen but came when he saw Clayton offering a sugar cube. Clayton fitted the harness and led the mule down the path in the full, clouded dark.

A sunless dawn brought a chill wind and slashing rain, and still, they worked: Clayton digging, Mr. Ed straining against the ropes, until finally the boat came free of the sand and began sliding over the hard pack. The mule hauled the boat into the surf and cleared the first breakers before Clayton untied the bowline and released him back to shore. Clayton lowered the outboard motor and pulled the cord. Rotten from years in the elements, it snapped. He took up the oars and somehow managed to fit them into the locks and keep the boat pointed into the surf. He had no strength for this, but a rip current had developed with the storm and carried the boat down shore and out, and soon it had cleared the roil and it pitched and yawed in the swell. He thought that he should set his net. Or bait the crab pots. He was content to weigh the possibilities, to enjoy the toss of the sea. The skiff leaked badly through chinked and cracked caulking, and he laughed at the sight and feel of his socks sponging the seawater rising from the boat's flooring. Where was his net, his gear? He looked back to shore, and there, in the distance, stood his mule, stone-frozen, watching, waiting for his sugar cube.

OLD INJURIES

The hard pack at the water's edge lay bare, the sand wind-swept clean, the sea a boiling gray, the brisk morning air slashed with rain and brine. Wade Whitcomb Jr. raced the All-Terrain Vehicle along the empty beach without having to worry about scattering sunbathers or frightening children. Junior worked for the Department of Beach Safety and Animal Control in Sand Point, Virginia. "Dog shit patrol," his father Wade Sr. had pronounced when years ago Junior had shown up at a family cookout, proud in his new, starched khaki uniform. But Junior liked his work: ticketing for open containers, unleashed and unruly pets, littering; providing first aid for minor cuts and scrapes; busting underage drinking parties; rounding up loose and injured animals for transport to a shelter or to the Sea Life Rehabilitation Center; tracking and eliminating the occasional rabid skunk or raccoon. At forty-three, with a thickening middle, a bum knee from an old football injury, and a chronically sore back from who knows what, Junior still enjoyed performing the mundane but necessary chores that kept the beach clean and safe, the tourists happy, and the Chamber of Commerce pleased with the flow of tourist dollars into Sand Point.

Junior had not been bothered by the dispatch call that came in just before six that morning. He'd been up for over an hour, awakened by that stupid nightmare that came every time storms brewed over the Atlantic. And there was no one other than himself to disturb at that early hour. He was alone now, living in a one-bedroom apartment four blocks from the ocean. He'd come close, twice, to marrying. Once in his thirties, but she declined his proposal and moved on, and again, just last year, when it had been his turn to end it. Afterward, he decided that as much as it hurt to have your heart broken, it hurt more to break one, and that it might be best to avoid either possibility for a while. At least, that is what he told himself.

So, awake and caffeinated, he was quick to respond to the report about an animal in possible distress. He hoped to find something exotic the storm blew in—a beached loggerhead, perhaps, or a stranded bottlenose dolphin, disoriented and huffing. But, no. The mule. Again. He came upon it standing still as a sand sculpture in the spume of the shore break. Junior eased the ATV close, cut the engine, dismounted, approached the mule, and patted its neck. "What is it this time, Mr. Ed?" The animal's ear twitched but it did not turn its gaze. He and the mule were well acquainted. It belonged to Clayton Royster, the old man who had a cottage in among the scrub oak behind the second dune line, near the brackish bay on the far side of the peninsula. Mr. Ed had been with Clayton for as long as Junior could remember and was now gray around the muzzle and swaybacked. The pair had been part of legend in Sand Point since Junior had been a youngster—the eccentric hermit and his sidekick.

To Junior, Clayton seemed neither eccentric nor especially reclusive, just an old man, neither friendly nor unfriendly, going about his business, earning a living from the sea by supplying roadside stands and local markets with fresh fish and crabs. When Junior had become serious about football during his freshman year in high school, not because he loved the sport but because his father did, he used to pass Clayton while running the beach on summer mornings to build the calves, the glutes. No matter how early Junior got out, Clayton was there before him, surfcasting or launching his boat to drop crab pots and set nets. He'd nod as Junior ran by, raise a finger to his cap sometimes, and Junior would wave back.

Through the years, Clayton appeared to age not at all. He was ancient back then and he was ancient now, the creases on his face perhaps a bit deeper, the skin more leathered. The same old Clayton, except for the mind. It was clear to Junior that Clayton had begun to misfire, like an ill-tuned outboard motor, a sputtering here and there, a sticky piston. And more and more frequently, Clayton displayed general disregard for social conventions. Junior reluctantly had been obligated to cite him for city code infractions—allowing Mr. Ed free rein of the beach during busy times, surfcasting his hooks and weights in among the bathers. As much as Junior took satisfaction in busting the litterers and the rowdy, sun-harshened crowds that raised hell on weekends, he did not enjoy prohibiting Clayton from doing what had been his lifework for decade upon decade.

Until recent years, Mr. Ed had helped Clayton haul his skiff into and out of the surf, pull the net, and cart away the catch. Clayton long ago could have replaced the mule with electric winches mounted on a sand-customized truck. Despite his workaday appearance, the Carhartt overalls and flannel work shirts, Clayton owned the section of oceanfront where they stood, the last undeveloped sand for miles in either direction. He could have sold out, become wealthy overnight, but he did not. He continued to work the water as he always had, continued to live in his rough quarters, and rather than judge him a fool as most in Sand Point did, Junior accepted Clayton's decision even though he didn't fully understand the reasoning behind it. To forgo the million and a half, or more, the property would command? Junior made do on a civil servant's paycheck. But being someone who had always dreamed of carving success from a world that seemed indifferent to his strivings, Junior wondered if Clayton was proiding an example to him: hard work and simple self-reliance can get you by just fine. Wade Sr., on the other hand, had dismissed Clayton as a "nutcase."

The mule and the man were both retired now, for the most part, except when Clayton would get in his head that he ought to take the boat out once more, and Junior would intercept them on the beach to dissuade the notion and to remind him that for the past few years the boat had rested half buried and rotting in the sand.

Junior absently ran his hand from the mule's neck to his fore shoulder and felt the wet leather of a harness and scolded himself for not noticing it earlier. He fingered the leather and followed the mule's gaze. The rain, a heavy curtain, gauzed his vision, but squinting, he believed he saw something on the horizon, an object bobbing, disappearing and reappearing with the rise and fall of the swells like a ghost in the spindrift, an apparition.

"Can't be," he said to the mule. He spun around searching for the boat by the dune line. "No way." Junior shook his head in denial even as he registered the shovel beside the pit, the gouge marks from dragging, and the harness draped from the mule's breastplate. He could not imagine how Clayton could have managed to disinter the boat from its grave, how the rickety structure could have held together while being pulled over the sand and pounded by the surf, nor, given the miracle of its resurrection, how the decrepit hulk might still prove seaworthy. He grabbed binoculars from the storage compartment on the ATV, and focusing, confirmed the craft unfit. Its hull barely showed above waterline and it listed dangerously. A figure Junior knew must be Clayton looked to be bailing, a repetitive pumping motion like a wind-up doll, a comical sight except for the disaster it foretold.

Junior called in the emergency but saw no way the boat could stay afloat until the cutter arrived, or even for the time it might take to organize a land-based rescue operation. A quarter mile down the beach in the direction the riptide carried the boat a red flag signaled an unattended lifeguard stand. He pushed the ATV full throttle to the stand, took his bolt cutters to the cable lashing the ten-foot rescue board to the platform's legs, cut the lock from the storage bin, removed a red foam torpedo buoy, and strapped it to the board through the handholds on the rail. At water's edge he kicked off his shoes, stripped to his underwear, tucked the board under his arm, and ran into the churn. Immediately, the surf slammed him, the cold took his breath, and the undertow unbalanced him. The following wave toppled him altogether, and saltwater flushed his nose and throat. All this not two yards from shore. Sputtering, gagging, he staggered to dry ground, stood and looked out. He reconsidered. In truth, an angry sea frightened him. A sane and rational person did not willingly enter it. As long as he had acted on instinct and adrenaline, he moved ahead of his fear. But once paused long enough for deliberation to overtake instinct, he froze. He was not an experienced lifeguard. Wait for backup. Monitor the situation. Don't foolishly act alone. Still.

FIFTEEN YEARS EARLIER, a storm reminiscent of this one. A rookie on patrol, he came upon three young teens, two boys and a girl, screaming for him. "There," they pointed.

The shore break deafening, at first he did not understand them. "She's out there." The surf zone seethed and frothed, the wind chop a white foamed and churning cauldron.

First lesson of sea rescue—establish visual contact. "Where?" Junior shouted.

They pointed again. "Frank dared her," one of the boys said. Junior studied the water. "I don't see anything." He scanned the beach in both directions for help. Red flags, beach closed, lifeguard stations unattended. "Did not," the other boy answered. Junior unsheathed the walkie-talkie from his hip, punched the talk button, and called for backup. "Do something," the girl stomped the sand. One of the boys jumped into the backwash of a breaker and scrambled back. "There," came a voice, and Junior thought he saw something too, an arm, flailing. As he stepped forward a wave almost buckled him, and when he regained balance and looked out, nothing. Had he seen the girl, or imagined her? Should he begin a search? What point of entry? What direction the current? His indecision anchored him in place. The sea stared him down, and won. He remained standing knee deep in the shore break, unmoving, until the rescue squad arrived and deployed into the surf.

Junior was part of the recovery team two days later when the girl washed ashore. Thirteen years old, she went into the water on a dare, only to her thighs, but the undertow waited, full of surprise and power. The rip. When they found her, the crabs had gotten to her, were on her still. Had he seen her waving for help? She had blonde hair; it would have blended in with the sea foam, wouldn't it? If he'd spotted her, made a positive ID, he would have gone in. He would have.

Junior had not eaten a crab since. Just the thought triggered his gag reflex.

HE'D LEARNED A LOT SINCE that first rescue attempt, of course. He knew immediately to call in the emergency, to locate and ransack the nearest lifeguard station for flotation equipment, and to strip off burdensome clothing. What he had not absorbed was how to take that first step into danger without overthinking, without hesitating. Wade Sr. used to lecture him about sports, "Don't think, react!" Junior could not, was unable to blank out visions of catastrophe: the rescue board ripped from him in the breakers; the boat sinking while he struggled to reach it; or, worse, arriving so exhausted from the swim he's incapable of providing aid, now two idiots requiring rescue, or recovery. It made no sense. Junior was beach patrol, damn it. Beach. This was not his fucking job. But he'd not gone in for the girl, and how had that worked out? She continued to haunt his dreams.

In the time spent deliberating, the boat had drifted farther out and down current. Junior tucked the board under his arm and took off running toward an entry point that would allow a favorable intercept angle. After only a few strides, his right knee locked up completely. It radiated pain and would not bend. He tried dragging the useless limb but stopped after a few steps, set down the equipment and began massaging life back into the damn knee.

A SHORT HISTORY OF THE DAMN KNEE: football, hit high from one side, low from the other, and pop. Following rehab, he tried to redeem himself at a two-year college but tore the ACL a second time during practice when he planted a foot to make a pivot. Again, he rehabilitated, not for himself, but for his father. Wade Sr. had played for the Bear at Alabama—rarely got on the field except on special teams where players were as expendable as cordwood, but he lived the honor of playing for the Bear his entire life, cherished the aches and pains that robbed him of sleep, the arthritis in his hips and broken fingers, the six concussions that muddled his memory and his speech, cherished it all, and expected his sons to embrace their pain as well.

Junior's rehabilitation had not gone well. The knee healed imperfectly, alternately locking on him or going wobbly. He feared the more permanent disability his father's presence testified to—so he quit the sport. Thereafter, he sensed a barrier like a seawall rise between him and his father. Junior's mother, who had never attended a game, out of disinterest, Junior assumed in his youthful ignorance, cried with relief when he announced his retirement from football, while his father turned his attention to two younger, still malleable, and able-bodied, sons. Junior attempted to set career goals. But the knee disqualified him in turn from the Navy and the police academy. Finally, after knocking around in sales, for which he was by temperament uniquely unqualified, he landed the job with the city—Department of Beach Safety and Animal Control. "Dog shit patrol," Wade Sr. had summarized, and punched Junior's arm. "Just kidding."

JUNIOR KNEADED THE LIGAMENTS at the back and side of his knee, rubbed his kneecap, flexed, tested his range of motion. Function restored, he gathered his equipment, filled his lungs, ran to his intercept point, and reentered the water. The first set of waves tried to rip the board from his grip, but he held on. Again he fought the waves, finally clearing the shore break. He slid onto the board in the relative calm of the trough between the inner and outer sandbars and paddled. Salt water stung his eyes, the ocean roiled and churned sand and seaweed, and as he made for deep water what struck him was how quiet the sea had grown, the roar of the shore break a distant resounding. Farther out, the waves broke inconsistently, a whooshing, and the board rose on swells and dipped into troughs. The silence made him feel somehow more isolated, more vulnerable, and he had to force down the rising panic pounding his heart, worming into his imagination, the crabs waiting below.

As he paddled, the muscles in his shoulders and back began to ache, and after what seemed to him a considerable time he sat upright to take bearings, legs straddling the board. The shore seemed distant, the dunes a vague sage green against a bruised sky, but seaward, not twenty yards ahead, the boat still floated and Clayton still bailed, scooping water over the transom with a blue coffee can. Junior waved both arms above his head and shouted, but Clayton did not turn from his efforts. Junior resumed paddling, pulled close, and again called out. Clayton glanced up, and then straightened and regarded Junior with wide eyes. "Junior, that you?" His voice hoarse, he coughed and spit into the water.

Junior took hold of the boat rail. "You OK, Clayton?" Droplets of rain or sweat or both beaded the stubble on the old man's face, gray hair hung limply from the hood of his yellow slicker, and his hands were white with cold and wrinkled from bailing. Inexplicitly, he wore no shoes, only black socks.

"What in the world are you doing out here in this weather?" Clayton asked.

"I'll be damned," was all Junior could manage.

"You'd best get into some warm clothes," Clayton said, pointing at Junior, naked save for his boxers. Suddenly, Junior had never been so cold in his life. The paddling had warmed him, but now he began to shiver.

"I need you to come onto this board here." Junior fought to keep his tone calm and firm with an authority he did not feel.

Clayton eyed the long, thin strip of fiberglass. "I'd rather sit out the storm right here," he said. "Get her bailed a little, and I think I can row. Get back to my fishing."

"I need you on this board," Junior's voice rose. "Can you swim?"

"Why do I need to swim? I have the boat." Clayton rapped on the rail.

The cold began to spasm the muscles of Junior's legs and arms, and a tightening in his chest forced quick and shallow breathing. "Can. You. Swim?" he repeated.

"Haven't had the occasion to for a while." Clayton scooped water.

"When? When was the last time you swam?"

"Can't recall."

A wave broke over the stern, and the boat settled to the waterline. Junior searched the horizon for sign of the Coast Guard cutter. Nothing. He slid from the board and pushed it alongside the gunwale. The water turbid and unknowable, the air rank with the odor of seaweed and decaying fish, he had to fight the urge to climb back on.

"Just ease over the side and onto this board here," he said, tamping down his desperation. "You need to get out of that heavy coat and those trousers first."

"What in hell for? I'm not taking off my clothes in public."

"Clayton, it's just the two of us," Junior said, voice rising. "And I'm already in my damn boxers."

Another swell washed over the seaward gunwale.

"You are sinking," Junior shouted. "I don't have time to debate." He smacked the board.

Clayton started, squinted at Junior as if just noticing his presence, and seemed at that moment to awake from a dream, to realize he literally sat in the ocean on the wooden plank of his stern seat. He dropped the coffee can he was holding, pulled the hood of his rain slicker tight around his head, snapped the top fastener, and attempted to scoot from his seat over the side rail of the boat and onto the rescue board. Junior tried to steady the board but it flipped, dumping Clayton into the sea.

"Here," Junior called, holding out the red foam floatation tube strapped to the board. Clayton instinctively reached for Junior rather than the float, latching onto his outstretched arm, pulling himself up and pushing Junior underwater. Junior found himself submerged before he had a chance to take a breath, and as Clayton struggled to hoist himself onto the rescue board using Junior for leverage, Junior fought the overwhelming urge to gasp for air, felt his lungs pushing, his throat opening, and then he fought Clayton, twisting at his hold, kicking at him, pounding at him with both fists, the water density robbing power but creating sufficient separation for him to jerk away. He surfaced, wild with panic, latched onto the RFD bobbing beside him, and sucked air. Huge, gulping, chest filling, life giving breaths. He shimmied onto the board and began wildly to paddle for shore. But, with oxygen and with the security of the board came relief, and with relief came awareness of where he was, and why. He sat up, his legs scissoring, a circle, and alongside the boat he spotted the yellow rain slicker floating just below the surface. He clutched a fistful of it, and miraculously Clayton remained enfolded within. Dropping from the board, draping his arm over the RFD, Junior held Clayton with one hand and guided him to the paddleboard and clumsily pushed and pulled him aboard. Clayton was uncommunicative but conscious, blue-faced but breathing, sputtering, and somehow able to maintain his hold on the board's side straps while Junior kicked for shore.

LATER, WRAPPED IN A MYLAR hypothermia blanket, Junior watched the ambulance crew attend to Clayton: exposure, a lung full of saltwater, contusions and scrapes, but otherwise in remarkably stable condition.

"We need to get you assessed at the hospital," the crew lead explained to Clayton. "Just to make sure." She was a tall woman named Evie who moved with smooth efficiency and whose voice conveyed a calm authority that Junior envied. He knew her from past encounters and recently had tried to screw up the nerve to ask her out. Standing there in his soaking boxers, the waistband squeezing a slight paunch, and draped in Mylar, he was pretty sure that now he never would.

Clayton shook his head. "No time. Things to attend to."

"They need to check you out," Junior said. "Don't be ornery."

"My mule," Clayton said.

"I'll take care of him," Junior said. "See that he gets back to your place, fed."

Evie glanced at Junior. "You should come with us too."

"I'm fine. Just need to get into some dry clothes," Junior said.

"Men," Evie said.

As they lifted Clayton onto the gurney and moved toward the ambulance, he held up a hand and motioned Junior close.

"You'll be fine," Junior said.

"My skiff," Clayton said.

"What about it?"

"Where is it?"

"My guess?" Junior began harshly, and then caught himself and tried to emulate Evie's composure. "I think that a few planks may wash up on this beach in a day or two. A few more eventually somewhere south, the Outer Banks maybe. The rest? Who knows?"

Clayton seemed to digest the speculation, mull it. "I should have kept bailing," he concluded, lifting his head from the gurney, looking out over the water. "I think the seas are starting to lie down."

Junior pulled on his clothes, wet and clammy from the rain, sat for his shoes, stood with his hind end coated in sand, draped his foul weather jacket over his shoulders, and handed the Mylar blanket to Evie. She took it, climbed into the ambulance, and eased away. Junior watched it move unhurriedly toward the pull-off onto the road, lights flashing but siren quiet. He mounted his ATV and considered heading home to change and warm up, but before he had a chance even to crank the engine, he saw Clayton's mule, Mr. Ed, lumbering toward him.

"Watched the drama, did you?" Junior asked when it drew close. Mr. Ed went to the indentation in the sand where Junior and Clayton had waited for the ambulance and pressed its muzzle low, and snorted. Junior needed to get dry, but he'd promised Clayton.

"Well, damn it all," he said, taking the rope hanging from the halter. He remounted the ATV and led Mr. Ed slowly along the beach and through the dune break, and up the twisting, unpaved, vine strewn drive leading to Clayton's cottage in among the thickets blanketing the higher, second line of sand dunes. Mr. Ed's pen stood at the back reach of the property. Mud and muck sucked at Junior's shoes, but under the lean-to dry straw covered the ground and a large feed pail held grass pellets. The mule went to the pail and began to eat.

Cold and miserable, Junior approached his ATV, paused, walked onto the screened-in front porch, tested the door, and found it unlocked. He removed his shoes, left them on the porch, and opened the door. Considering the disarray of Clayton's yard, the rust-pocked truck at the head of the drive, the cardboard boxes stacked under the overhang on his side wall, the PVC pipes scattered about, the assortment of motor parts littering the front porch, and the stinking pen out back, inside he expected to be assaulted by the sights and smells of a loner on the decline: the funk of an old man's indifferent attention to hygiene, a stack of unwashed dishes reeking of three-day fish scraps, the mildewed air heavy with decay. Instead, he found a tidy, if sparely furnished front room containing a recliner worn at the armrests, a sofa with a pillow at one end and a folded flannel blanket at the other, a small TV on what looked to be a homemade stand, and a dining table holding not dinnerware but fishing gear, mostly reels, some partially disassembled, neatly laid out on several layers of newspaper and smelling of bearing oil. He was drawn to the kitchen by the still lingering aroma of coffee. The pot was cold but he turned up the flame on the gas stove and by the time he located a cup, searched the refrigerator for a splash of milk, and the cupboard for sugar, it was hot enough so that he cherished the warmth that flowed from his throat into his stomach as he drank. After downing a second cup, he rinsed it in the sink and walked back into the main room. The place spoke to a well-ordered, simple life. Neat. Snug.

Junior was surprised by his discoveries, perhaps expecting to see something in Clayton's surroundings that reminded him of his father's decline. As Wade Sr. had settled more deeply into dementia, he cared nothing about bathing or changing out of soiled clothing, and Junior's mother found it impossible to manage a large man with increasingly unpredictable emotions, the brooding silences and red-faced fits of rage, the breaking of dishes, throwing of food. Junior and his brothers helped when they could, but toward the end, his mother couldn't keep up, and his childhood home became a smelly mess, a dump. When Wade Sr. failed to wake one morning three years ago, Junior gave thanks and told anyone who asked that football had killed his father, more than forty years after playing his final game.

But, no, Clayton was not Wade Sr., and even given his mental lapses, Clayton was more alive at eighty-something than Wade Sr. had been at sixty-five. Junior examined the fishing gear laid out on the dining table, picked up a reel, felt its heft, ran a finger along the protective film of oil coating its surface. Clayton remained living in the moment, planning his next outing, fully engaged. Alone but seemingly not lonely.

And Junior. Was he lonely? Content? He lived in town, had many acquaintances. But no one close. His neighbors tended to come and go, most were in the Navy, and he knew them only by occasional two-sentence greetings by the mailbox and by the sounds that seeped through the shared wall: the too-loud video games, the bathroom fan, the occasional thumping from the bedroom. So, in one sense he was as isolated as Clayton, but standing there in Clayton's cottage, something felt different. Clayton belonged to this place, and this place belonged to Clayton. The man, the cottage, the sea, and, yes, the mule, all part of the whole. Junior went out into the rain.

Back at his apartment, after a hot shower that drained the tank cold, he sat in front of the TV flipping channels and sipping hot tea mixed with the juice of half a lemon. His head felt wrapped in a compression bandage, and his knee throbbed. He thought back over the day, as he would for years to come. He had fought off Clayton, had pushed him away. He knew in his bones that he would have left him to drown if the rescue board had not been at hand. He'd failed completely the girl years ago and nearly failed Clayton today. But in the end, he had not. He'd thought to bring the equipment from the lifeguard stand. He'd fended off the terror. He'd done his job. Was that good enough? Might Wade Sr. have thrown a backhanded compliment his way? "I guess you finally finished something you started." Junior hoped so. He wanted to feel good about himself. He wished he had someone to talk it over with. His knee ached. He wished he had someone.

GIDDY'S PET & PLAY

It had rained hard the day before, with gusting winds that stripped leaves from trees, rattled shutters, and brought a chill unusual for early September in Sand Point. Giddy Cobb stood at the kitchen window looking out at the barn and the playground, making mental notes of the work that did not get done yesterday. And today, the mud-slicked corral and the water-pooled lawn would slow progress. Giddy was fifty-five years old and had just ended her twenty-eighth season operating Giddy's Pet & Play. She was closing for the winter, as she did every year following Labor Day. It always brought on reflection and melancholy, a sense of loss and the anticipation of the long, quiet months ahead before she reopened on Memorial Day weekend. She would miss the tourists—most people on holiday presented a softer-edged, lighter version of themselves, and she enjoyed being around them. She had become friends with several who made Sand Point an annual vacation tradition, had watched children grow and marriages begin and end.

When she woke that morning to a clearing sky, her initial impulse was to comb the beach for what the storm deposited: driftwood in interesting configurations or newly deposited shells. She once found a Portuguese fishing buoy, a cobalt blue glass orb wrapped in gray netting. But work called. She was behind schedule. So, Giddy put aside her walk and instead went outside to the barn, grabbed a crescent wrench from the tool bin, called "Hello babies," to her animals, and continued on to the playground. She couldn't have equipment sitting around unattended during the offseason. "Attractive nuisance," they called it, and should someone wander in and break an arm, a child possibly, but more likely some teens fueled with malt liquor, they could sue you from here to forever.

She planned to disassemble the merry-go-round for storage, but when she fitted the wrench to the bolt holding the deck assembly to the center pole, it refused to loosen. She placed a foot on the edge of the deck, gripped the wrench with both hands, and leveraged her weight against the unyielding bolt. Nothing. "I don't need this today." She tossed the wrench onto the deck with disgust, metal clanging on metal. When she turned toward the barn to retrieve the can of WD-40, she noticed one of her goats, Ninny, wobbling in tight circles in the middle of the corral. As Giddy approached, Ninny began bleating, high-pitched and plaintive. Giddy draped an arm around the goat's neck to stop its aimless, unsteady circling. "Whoa girl, easy there." She checked the animal's eyes, which looked clouded, and gently prodded her belly, which felt slightly distended. A musty odor rose off her, ammonia tinged.

Giddy hated this part of the business, a sick animal. Ninny was her favorite goat, a calm Toggenburg, friendly with the children but sufficiently sturdy and willing to pull a small wagon holding two or three toddlers around the corral.

"It's OK, girl, you'll be fine." Giddy guided the goat to her stall inside the barn and added feed and fresh water, which

Ninny sniffed before flopping onto her straw bedding. Giddy stood beside her for a moment and took note of the rapid rise and fall of her chest, the wheezing. "OK, rest first, and then food."

She returned to the playground and sprayed the uncooperative bolt with WD-40. Retrieving her wrench, she noted chipped paint from the merry-go-round deck where she had tossed it. "Thanks, Giddy." Another chore to add to the list. She gave everything a fresh coat each spring, but she'd have to prime the mars so rust wouldn't set in over the damp of winter. She tapped the bolt with the wrench and when she set her weight against it, it released so easily she stumbled backwards. She began assembling the tripod hoist she used to help with heavy lifting when a white Beach Safety & Animal Control truck pulled into the lot and Junior Whitcomb climbed out and walked towards her. He'd not been around this season. He looked good: maybe a few pounds heavier, but his frame could handle it. His hair, sun-bleached from a summer's worth of outside work was surely longer than regulation. He walked with a hitch, and old football injury, and Giddy wondered if his knee might be acting up again. He was, now, about the age she had been when they first met.

"Look what the storm blew in," Giddy said, smiling. "I wondered when you'd get by."

Junior dipped his head. "Hi Giddy." He tapped the thick citation book sticking from his back pocket. "Just the annual reminder about unattended animals."

"You shouldn't sit on that when you drive," Giddy said, pointing to the book. "I've told you I don't know how many times. Throw your back all out of whack."

At the end of each season, an accumulation of animals had outgrown the Pet & Play and were no longer cuddly or friendly to the toddlers. Over the years, Giddy had developed a barter system of sorts. The local organic egg man took her hens in exchange for chicks the following spring, and an artesian creamery took her yearling lambs and the unruly goats and provided newly weaned animals when time came to reopen the Pet & Play. But sometimes she could not find a trade, and she hated the idea of consigning her rabbits and piglets to the fur farm and feed lot, so occasionally over the years Animal Control would get a call about a garden overrun with floppy eared creatures or a pig wandering the pine marsh.

Junior glanced around the lot. "Another season come and gone. Hard to believe."

Giddy ran a finger along the merry-go-round deck, noticing several other areas that needed priming. Indeed, another season come and gone. "Give me a hand with this thing?" They stood opposite one another and gripped the side of the round deck. "Ready?" she said, and for a moment they regarded one another straight on, and then Junior dropped his eyes.

"Ready," Junior said, and they lifted in unison. "Good Lord," he said, when they had hoisted the deck from the post.

"Heavier than it looks," Giddy said. They tilted the deck on edge, and their hands brushed. "I was sorry to hear about you and Shelby," she said. Shelby and Junior had been together for over a year, and most townsfolk assumed they'd be married sooner rather than later. But several months ago, Junior had broken it off. No one really knew why. Junior shrugged. "Sometimes things just don't work out. No one's fault."

She flushed. In so many words, that is what she had told Junior fifteen years earlier, after she'd ended things. He'd stopped by the Pet & Play to introduce himself, a rookie to the Animal & Beach Patrol. It was 1997. She had been about to turn forty and wondering if she might be going to seed, and he was twenty-eight, she later learned, broad-shouldered with muscular arms and commonplace handsome features, a prominent nose that looked as if it might have once been broken, wide-set eyes, strong chin. Yet she sensed a vulnerability that attracted her, the way he approached with his head dipped, a slight but noticeable limp, and his soft and unassertive tone. "Please don't let loose any more pigs," he had asked that first meeting. "They go feral, turn mean. I'll just have to shoot them, and I would not like that." He'd overstayed the "official" visit and she had openly flirted with him just to test the waters. She possessed a trim figure kept well toned with work, chestnut-colored hair that tended to look wild and slept in, and hazel eyes that could hold you captive when she wanted. Yet, after a certain age you began to wonder.

They rolled the deck into the barn and stood looking at the menagerie—the hens and ducks, the two ponies another year older. "My babies," Giddy said. Junior noticed Ninny in her bed. She tried to rise when they entered, gathered her legs under her, but collapsed. "He seems a little sickly," Junior said

"She," Giddy corrected.

"She," Junior said. "She looks peaked." They stood watching the goat for a moment.

"She was fine yesterday, and this morning could hardly walk."

"Maybe you should get Lisa to look her over?"

The vet. One of the first persons Giddy met when she moved to Sand Point, her best friend and her most burdened creditor. "Maybe," Giddy answered.

"Well," Junior said, stepping toward the corral.

"Thanks for the help," Giddy said, and then impulsively, "Have time for a cup of coffee? Tea? Catch up a little?"

Junior paused, seemed to consider the invitation. "No, I guess not. Someone called about an injured hawk in their backyard."

"Of course. I have tons to get done myself."

Giddy watched Junior walk back to his truck. He had proposed marriage back then. Imagine that. It had caught her by surprise, and she had answered instinctively and a little brusquely. "Don't be silly," and after the pain registered in his eyes, she softened. "It's not you. Sometimes things just don't fit. No one's fault. You need to find someone your own age, have a bunch of babies, bring them here and spend a lot of money on candy and cart rides." She tried to laugh, but when he blanched at her false gaiety she stopped trying to ease the sting. Months later, after Junior had recovered from his hurt, they'd begun a cautious friendship that gradually deepened. Sand Point was a small town, after all, and the benefits of getting along outweighed the complications of avoidance and acrimony. And, Giddy genuinely liked Junior, perhaps even loved him. But after Junior and Shelby became a couple, his visits grew less regular, and now Giddy realized how much she had missed not seeing him around.

"I'm in Sand Point for another few days," she called to him. "If you find time."

Junior raised a hand but did not turn. He climbed into his truck and pulled from the lot. Giddy stood in the corral as the truck disappeared around the curve leading into Sand Point and wondered for maybe the hundredth time over the years if she'd made a mistake turning Junior away so many years ago. She'd never had trouble attracting male attention, but, until Junior, she'd chosen poorly. Married at nineteen, divorced at twenty-one, married *and* divorced at twenty-six. Her fatally flawed men were in her eyes as lovable as puppies, and salvageable, right up until they proved her wrong. She'd married young to escape home, and ended up with a carbon copy of her father and brother: lazy and verbally abusive. Her second husband was hardworking and friendly, easy on the eyes, and loving…oh so loving. To everyone. Everyone! But, with Junior, perhaps she'd chosen wisely and failed to recognize it.

Giddy returned to the playground and removed the seats from the swing set, undraped, folded, and stored the red, white, and blue bunting from the fence rails, and worked a bit on winterizing the machinery. But she moved sluggishly, without enthusiasm, and whittled away the afternoon. She went to the barn to check again on Ninny, who did not appear to have stirred since mid-morning. She sat on a hay bale and rubbed Ninny's ears and her two other goats and the lamb yearling came over and nuzzled her, begging treats. Chickens pecked at her feet, and she talked to them. "Easy street for you guys," she told them. She explained that she'd arranged board for the some of them until next spring, and new homes for the others. "Not so easy for me," she added. Soon, she would make the six-hour drive west to winter over at her childhood home and help around the house for room and board. The Pet & Play had allowed Giddy self-reliance, but it never prospered beyond a hand-to-mouth operation. Years past, she'd remained offseason in Sand Point and got by working part-time at the outlet stores over the holidays. But with the turn of the new century, business noticeably slowed when the older kids, the pre-teens, discovered Game Boys and cell phones and begun disappearing into an imaginary digital world more exciting to them than the physical one. And, for the past several years, since the economic "bubble" burst for reasons Giddy found unfathomable, offseason work had burst as well, and when her power was cut in 2008 during a cold snap that froze her pipes and sickened a few of the animals, she'd made plans to winter with her aging parents and useless brother at their small farm, helping with the pumpkin and persimmon harvest to sell at the autumn farmer's markets and holiday festivals, and saving on food and utilities during the lean months. Just until the economy picked up, she consoled herself.

But the economy was slow to recover. Jobs remained scarce. Two years ago, her parents quit farming, a combination of failing health and tired land, the persimmon trees, like her parents, well past their prime, old and diseased, and almost barren of fruit. So, for the past two visits there had been nothing to occupy her time other than menial housework and cooking: pork and potatoes, beef and potatoes, maybe a roasted chicken. And potatoes. Winter lasted an eternity.

Giddy sat with her animals a while longer and tossed a handful of cracked corn onto the barn floor and watched the chickens scramble and peck. She tried to get Ninny interested in a few handheld food pellets but could not. She returned to the house to call Lisa, the veterinarian, but could not find her cell phone, which she was forever misplacing. She was about to expand her search to the barn when ringing came from somewhere in the kitchen and she found the phone in the laundry basket tucked into the back pocket of jeans waiting for the washer.

"That you, Gladys?" Only her family called her by her birth name, even when, as a teen, she stopped answering to it. She remained silent.

"It's Earl." Her brother lived in the converted basement of their parent's house, if you could call painting the cinder-block walls blue and tossing two braided throw rugs onto the concrete floor and roughing out a bathroom but leaving the drywall unfinished and the door unhung, "converted."

"Hello, Earl."

"Where are you? Expected you last week."

"Weather put me behind," Giddy lied.

"Dad hoped you'd get the alfalfa mowed." Although they'd given up farming, the pasture would yield for another year or two until the weeds took over.

"I have a sick animal." That part was true.

"Alfalfa's ready."

"Thanks for understanding. I'll let you know when I'm headed out. Put Mom or Dad on to say hi."

After she'd hung up, she dialed Lisa and reported Ninny's symptoms. Lisa asked questions, offered to come out later that evening. It could be any number of things, including age.

Giddy mentally calculated what she must already owe Lisa for past services. She'd been a good and generous friend. "Let's wait a day or two."

"Your call," Lisa said, "but you know I don't mind a bit. I just have to wait until John gets home. I'm watching the kids." Lisa was a grandmother already, her daughter an attorney, something in employment relations, and Lisa watched the two children two days a week. Giddy momentarily pictured Lisa, her husband John, and the two toddlers eating mac-n-cheese and later watching whatever animated feature captured the current fascination of the young ones. It would almost certainly involve animals, not her kind but the other, the computer-generated kind. Lisa and John would be sipping wine, white probably. Giddy would not impose on that,

124 • GIDDY'S PET & PLAY

a pleasant, domestic evening, although her thoughts were conflicted. A part of her envied Lisa her life, her settled, successful practice, her settled, comfortable marriage, her motherhood, andand grand motherhood. Another part of her recoiled at the image. "Is that it? Is that all?" To be settled? The thought repelled her, may have been what drove her risky choice in men, her rejection of Junior. To be settled. Domestic.

"I'll keep close watch on Ninny," Giddy said. "I'll take notes and let you know if anything changes for the worse."

"Or for better," Lisa said.

"I'll let you get back to those grandkids," Giddy said.

"I thought you might have been calling about Clayton," Lisa said.

Clayton Royster, an old loner Giddy had met decades ago and come to like a great deal. "What about Clayton? " She couldn't help but think stroke or heart, because of his age.

"I can't believe you haven't heard."

"I'm listening, Lisa."

"He took his boat out in the storm yesterday and managed to sink it."

Giddy knew the boat. She had a habit of walking early before opening, and her favorite route took her along the beach for a mile or so until she reached Clayton's fishing boat partially buried in the sand. It hadn't been used in years, and she could not imagine how that hulk could have been launched, let alone kept afloat.

"Is he all right?"

"He's fine," Lisa said.

"Thank goodness."

"He thought to go fishing. In that wreck of his."

"I think he's slipping a little," Giddy said, and immediately regretted having given voice to her concern.

"Probably would have drowned if Junior hadn't come along."

"Wait! What? Junior?"

"Patrolling the beach, saw Clayton in distress, somehow managed to get to him on a rescue board he grabbed from the lifeguard stand."

"What the hell," Giddy said. "He was here just today. Didn't mention a thing."

"You know Junior," Lisa said. "He's not one to draw a lot of attention to himself."

Giddy thought about his limp earlier, wondered if he may have aggravated his knee during the rescue. She'd not asked about it. She'd been distracted by Ninny, and by chores. Still.

"Paramedics wanted them both checked out at the hospital," Lisa said. "They declined."

"What is it with men?" Giddy asked, not expecting an answer.

That evening, Giddy sat on the front porch watching evening come on and sucking on a cherry Popsicle. The crickets and frogs started up a high-pitched racket, and bats swooped for gnats and late season mosquitoes and whatnot. She had gotten to know Clayton Royster years ago when she sold him her mule, Eddie. Eddie had been with Giddy that first year of the Pet & Play, a mule foal just newly weaned. After a few seasons Eddie started to become, well, mulish. He was not a gentle ride for the kiddos, and sometimes he nipped. She no longer had a use for him but also had no idea how to put him to pasture. Her parents had declined to take him, suggested the processing plant. Thank God for Clayton Royster.

The old man, at least he seemed old to her then, although he seemed no older to her now, came to see her—she'd made it known around town she was looking for a new home for Eddie, and Clayton had need for his services. Giddy knew Clayton from her beach walks. He always seemed to be there, setting a net or surfcasting from the beach. She'd pause on her walk to watch him cast and she'd follow the silver lure as it flashed in the sun and plopped into the surf. Once, she watched him catch a bluefish and she had commented on its beauty, its torpedo shape, blue-green scales and pearl-white belly. He unhooked it and offered it to her commenting it might feed her for several meals. She had accepted, grasped the fish by its forked tail, avoiding the teeth, and placed it back into the ocean. Clayton had watched, removed his cap, scratched his head, and laughed.

That meeting had defined their relationship. He seemed amused by her, and she thought she understood him. He was a loner, but unlike some who soured on everyone and everything, Clayton's default temperament, once you got past his reticence, seemed to be one of bemused observation. And he spoke reverently of his surrounding, the physical world of the sea and the dunes, the bay and the bayside lowlands. So, when he came asking about Eddie, she offered him at a bargain price. She knew Clayton intended to use him as a workmate, but knew also there would never be a question of abuse.

The following morning, Ninny seemed neither better nor worse, and after a half-hearted stab at packing for her trip, Giddy drove to visit Clayton, and Eddie. On the hard-packed driveway that wound between low dunes and scrub thickets to Clayton's cottage, the foliage hinted at autumn. A fading in the green of the canopy, a tinge of red on the vines. Although his truck was parked in the clearing, no one answered when she called from the porch or when she knocked on the door. She walked around back and found Eddie beneath the shelter of the lean-to at one side of the pen. He looked up from his feed bucket when she unlatched the gate and he moved toward her as she approached.

"Hi Eddie," Giddy rubbed his muzzle and he nudged her. "How've you been, old boy?" After standing beside her for a moment, the mule returned to the feed bucket. Giddy took note of the nearly full bucket, clean water in the trough, fresh straw beneath the lean-to, and boot prints in the mud of the pen. She returned to the house, called once more, tried the knob, inched open the door and hollered, "Hello? Clayton?"

"Who's that?" a voice croaked from inside.

"It's Giddy Cobb."

"Well, come in then."

She found Clayton nested in his recliner and wrapped in a red-checkered blanket. The TV was on a fishing show but the sound was off. She sat on the sofa.

"How are you feeling?"

Clayton raised a hand to cover a cough. "Took a little dip yesterday."

"I heard." The man on the TV show hooked a bass, brought it into the boat, and kissed it. "I'd never be hugging on that man," Giddy said, and Clayton harrumphed and began coughing again, deep and chesty.

"Had my boat out fishing. Took a spill," Clayton said, when he'd recovered.

"In that weather," Giddy said. He looked sunken to her, older, and she wondered not for the first time exactly what his age might be. Eighty? Eighty-five? The stubble on his chin showed white.

"The boy was there to help me."

"Lucky for you," Giddy said.

"That Junior fella. Nice boy, but a little excitable."

"I'm going to make you some tea," Giddy said.

"No tea in the cupboard," Clayton said. "But I'd take coffee if you don't mind perking some up."

Giddy returned several minutes later with coffee for both of them and a plate of buttered toast for Clayton and set the mug and the toast on the small table beside his chair. Clayton worked the lever on the recliner to sit upright and took a sip of coffee. "Honestly, Clayton, I don't know what you were thinking. You could have died."

"Seemed like a good idea at the time," he said. "I've ridden lot rougher seas." He took a bite of toast, washed it down with coffee. "But those were younger days, sturdier boats."

"And Junior happened along, hauled you in?"

"He did. Came out on one of those long thingamajigs from the lifeguard shack to collect me."

Giddy thought back to when Junior had admitted that he loved the ocean but was wary of it.

"He looked pretty worked up out there," Clayton said, as if reading her mind. "But he came, and he took me to shore." Clayton began coughing again.

"You need to have that checked out."

"Already did. They thought maybe I should stay a day or two."

"Yet, here you are." Giddy spread her arms.

"Work to get done."

"I noticed Eddie has feed and water."

"Mr. Ed," Clayton corrected. When she had sold the mule to Clayton, he thought Eddie too childish a name for a full-grown work animal. At the time, some kidded him about naming the animal after a TV show, but Clayton had no idea what they were talking about.

"Well, you should listen to medical advice," Giddy said, and then as an afterthought, "I forgot to bring him a carrot. I always bring a carrot."

"Getting older," Clayton said, and Giddy was unsure whether he was referring to her, or to himself, or to Eddie.

"Yes," she said.

They sat there awhile in silence watching the soundless TV, now a new fishing show featuring a cruiser-sized fiberglass hulk glittering in a sun-drenched, turquoise sea.

"Does the sound work on that thing?" Giddy asked.

"Imagine a boat like that," Clayton said.

"I can't." She suspected it would cost twice what her house was worth, and considered for a moment whether what she felt toward the sun-bronzed, ruggedly handsome man driving it was envy or contempt.

"It works, but there's not much worth listening to," Clayton said.

Giddy stood and carried their cups and the plate into the kitchen and rinsed them in the sink. When she came back, Clayton seemed to be napping. She went to the door.

"They said I shouldn't be here alone," Clayton said.

Giddy stood with the door ajar. "Who? Who said you shouldn't?"

"They said I needed watching."

Giddy eased shut the door and returned to the couch.

"How do you feel about that?"

Clayton leaned toward her. "I forget things. I hate it. I go missing awhile, in my head, and I come back and there are these gaps. I just hate it."

"I forget where my keys are," Giddy said, helplessly. "Just yesterday…"

Clayton cut her short with a wave of his hand. "There's carrots in the garden."

"What?" Giddy wondered if he might be wandering.

"You said you forgot to bring Mr. Ed a carrot."

"Right," Giddy said, relieved. She stood, went again to the door.

"Don't like the idea of some stranger poking around my place, giving me pills I don't want and food I have no taste for," Clayton said.

"I can understand that. Maybe your son could help out?" Dan, lived inland and owned a car dealership. They weren't particularly close, Giddy knew, but neither were they estranged.

"Busy," Clayton said. "I'd never put him out like that."

"It could be the best option, if you gave him a chance." Giddy opened the door. "You take care, Clayton."

Clayton turned in his recliner and caught Giddy's eye. "I would have been all right out there," he said.

"Where?"

"The boat."

"The boat? You told me it was taking on water."

"It was. It sank."

"You could have drowned."

Clayton held Giddy's gaze and nodded. "That's what I just said. I would have been all right out there."

Giddy started to protest, but instead, after a moment of reflection to collect her thoughts, search for the right words, she realized the perfect logic of his reasoning. The sea, like going home. And the boat, perhaps his last, best opportunity to act on his own free will, to assert his independence. He may not have planned to end his life there and then, but he certainly would have been at peace with that outcome. "You take care of yourself, Clayton," she said. "I have need of you still."

"Don't forget those carrots," Clayton said, and leaned back in the recliner.

Giddy eased shut the door, walked to the garden, pulled two carrots unyieldingly from the sandy loam, went to the pen, fed them to Eddie and found herself leaning against him for support, her eyes misting. Clayton suddenly wizened, Eddie swaybacked with the weight of years, both white whiskered and vulnerable, and she, not yet old but clearly more than half her life behind her, the most promising half. Now comes the hanging on: to hope, to health, to vigor.

Returning home, Giddy checked on Ninny and found her dead. She did not mourn. She gave thanks that Ninny died in familiar surroundings among those of her kind. "Good," she said aloud. She flipped open her cell phone and called Junior for help with the disposal, said the next morning would be fine, no rush now. She desperately wanted to ask him about Clayton's ocean rescue, but fought the urge, perhaps because she was a little hurt that he obviously hadn't felt comfortable sharing his feelings earlier. And then she made another call to her basement brother, Earl, and paced the corral while explaining that she would not be home that winter, that he would have to see to the alfalfa field himself, that she had obligations here, would make do in Sand Point somehow, taking care of her critters. She ended the call in the midst of his protest.

Later, Giddy sat on the front porch in one of the rockers sipping chamomile tea as full night came on. Clouds obscured the moon, and lightening flashed within the clouds, illuminating them, and between them in thick jagged tendrils. She rose from the chair and switched off the lights inside and out and felt her way back to the rocker in inky darkness and watched the electricity spider-web across the heavens. The melancholy of the day gradually lifted. She lost herself in the vastness, felt very small yet, strangely, significant, as if her witnessing leant meaning to the display. She participated. At this moment, on this day, she felt fully alive, and hopeful.

She sat in the rocker for a minute, or an hour, alone in her thoughts until gradually the surrounding world reasserted itself: A bleat from the barn that reminded her of Ninny, cars occasionally passing on the road coming or going into Sand Point, dots of red or white, tires swooshing, the low thrum of engines. A truck slowed as it approached the Pet & Play, paused on the road, and turned into the lot, briefly capturing Giddy in the sweep of its headlamps. It came to a halt beside the house and went quiet and dark. In brief flashes of lightening, Giddy recognized Junior's profile behind the wheel. After some time, he exited and climbed the stairs onto the front porch. Giddy padded the arm of the Adirondack chair beside her and he sat.

"Want some tea?" Giddy asked. "A beer?"

"The other day, during the storm," Junior began, and stopped.

"I heard," Giddy said.

"I was so afraid. I almost turned back. More than once."

Giddy reached over and rested her hand on his forearm. "But, you didn't," she said. "You didn't turn back."

"I did not."

"Can you talk to me about it," she asked. "Please?"

TAKING STOCK

Clayton Royster, age eighty years and change, went into the sea four hundred yards off the beach in September of 2012 after his decrepit skiff floundered during a storm. He would have drowned had not Junior Whitcomb, a Sand Point Beach Safety Officer, happened by, spotted him, and fished him sputtering from the water. The dunking left Clayton with a bad cough that lingered, settled deep into his chest, and evolved into pneumonia. He entered the hospital early in October and spent gauzy days in a medicine and fever induced fog followed by a week regaining awareness in fits and starts, and another week in the rehab wing exercising his lungs and practicing to walk, tie his shoes, sit on the toilet and stand from it.

Before signing his release, the hospital insisted he undergo a few additional tests. A curly-haired man with a calm voice and a soft midsection led him into an office and motioned to a seat beside a gray metal table. The man, "Dr. Tad," according to his nametag, sat across the table from Clayton.

"You are almost ready for discharge," Tad explained. "We just have to make sure you are safe to return home."

"Safe from what?"

"Well, from yourself. From unhealthy thoughts."

So, that's what this is about, Clayton thought. He'd mentioned to his friend Giddy Cobb that he would have been OK with going down with the ship. And maybe to his son Dan as well. It would have been a fitting waterman's way to leave this world and relatively quick compared to the slow downward glide of the past few years. He had no idea how to express such thoughts, so he said nothing.

"Just a few tests," Tad said, after a pause. "First, I'd like you to listen to these words and try to remember them. Banana, sunrise, chair."

Clayton nodded. Stupid words. Nonsense.

"Now," Tad said. "A few questions." He straightened, tapped a pen on a legal pad, and leaned forward slightly. "How have you been feeling lately?"

Clayton wondered where Tad had come from. "I've had pneumonia. Cooped up in the hospital."

"Other than that, how have you been? Mentally? Depressed or anxious?"

"I've been in the hospital. Sick."

Tad made a note. "Have you been tired? Trouble sleeping?"

"Have you ever spent time in the hospital?" Clayton asked, agitated. "Of course I've had trouble sleeping."

Tad wrote something else in the pad. "Have you been feeling bad about yourself? Felt like you've let your family or yourself down?"

Clayton started to speak, and then went silent. Of course he'd let his family down. He'd been selfish, put his own needs and wants ahead of his family. Always. He'd been a poor father to Dan and a worse husband to Loretta. He'd neglected them both whenever the sea or the marsh bay called, which seemed always at times when family needed him most.

"No," he answered.

Dr. Tad made one final note and slid a blank paper across the table to Clayton, handed him a pencil, and asked him to draw a clock and set it to quarter past eleven. Clayton drew a circle and labeled the clock face and then looked up, waiting.

"Do you remember what time to set the clock?" Dr. Tad asked.

"Of course," Clayton said. "Do you want AM or PM?" Tad began to make a note before Clayton added. "Just pulling your leg," and drew the big hand pointing to the three and the small hand to just past the eleven. "You know," he said, "my son could never pass this test."

"Does he have cognitive issues?" Dr. Tad asked.

"No. He has digital. I don't think he ever owned a real timepiece."

"I see," Dr. Tad said, attempting a weak smile. "Can you remember the three words I gave you?"

"Yes."

"Can you repeat them for me?"

"Yes," said Clayton, and waited.

Dr. Tad made a note. "Would you like a hint?"

"No."

"Well, then?"

"Do you want them in order or just any old way?"

"Either will do."

"Banana, sunrise, chair," Clayton said. "Chair, sunrise, banana."

AND THEN NOVEMBER ARRIVED, delivering crisp mornings and a cold sun. Back in his cottage near the sea, Clayton's attempts to reestablish routine met with frustration. It was the time of the year to be fishing for puppy drum and speckles, but whenever he determined to collect his gear, load his mule Mr. Ed for the walk to the beach, dodge the traffic along the new blacktop the city had put through two years earlier, search for his boat that of course no longer was there, someone magically appeared to dissuade him. Junior Whitcomb might encounter him while patrolling the shoreline. "I'm not dredging you out of the surf again. Too cold." Or Giddy Cobb, who had sold Clayton her mule so long ago, would show up just as Clayton was leading Mr. Ed from his pen. "No. Eddie is retired. And so are you." Or his part-time day nurse, Samson Okafor, would arrive and tire him with rehab exercises and other quiet demands.

Clayton liked Samson, a compact, thick-framed man whose softly accented speech was so deep and low Clayton had to strain to understand him. Clayton's first inclination had been to dismiss Samson immediately. But when the man showed on at his porch, waiting outside until Clayton invited him in, recognizing the disassembled Penn reel laid out on the dining table for cleaning, commenting on his garden which still held late season potatoes and onions, Clayton could not help but accept Samson into his life, even if he did not understand why he might choose to enter it.

"You see folks at their worst," Clayton said. "I'm cranky sometimes."

"I enjoy helping out."

"Even if I don't want help? Even if I'd just as soon you depart this place so I can get on with my business?"

"I will. I will depart—just as soon as you finish these exercises, swallow your pills, and eat a little of that food sitting on the table someone took the time to prepare for you."

One morning near mid-November, Clayton woke early, sunrise still an hour away, dawn just beginning to seep into the room. He rose with an energy he'd not felt in weeks and managed to halter an unenthusiastic Mr. Ed. "No lollygagging," he scolded, and cajoled the mule from the pen and down the drive and across the blacktop and out onto the sand. Clayton dropped the halter and stood at water's edge as the sun crept from the pewter sea and scanned the deserted beach and looked out at the vast expanse of water, and realized he'd forgotten his gear, perhaps never intended to fish at all, and it came to him with piercing clarity that he never again would fish. So, it was all nearing an end. The fishing. The crabbing. Life. He was nervous about the prospect, and not wholeheartedly ready. But the world did not owe him one extra day. Not one.

Clayton had always been most at ease in his solitude. In truth, he'd never felt lonely until just recently when well meaning folks began showing up to care for him. They forced him to acknowledge what he'd forgone, what relationships he'd forfeited in exchange for the life he chose, and he stood in the sand as the rising tide began lapping at his feet and wondered if the cost had been worth it. The cold water roused him from his reverie, and he shooed away further thoughts, too late for such nonsense. He would not become an old man filled with regret. He stood awhile longer and breathed deeply the salt air, more therapeutic for him than all the spirometer exercises forced on him. This was his world, his heaven—the sea, the sand, the salt marsh. He did not know what came next, after this, but he was not quite ready to take leave of this current presence where his soul resided.

Clayton returned home exhausted and after seeing to Mr. Ed's needs settled into his recliner to nap. He slept so deeply that upon waking he couldn't remember the day or the place and at first thought he was still in the hospital tethered to the machines, and that the chatter he heard was the shift change, the nurses handing off information on his latest vitals, appetite, and bowel movements. But no, he was at home now, the realization came with relief, in his compact but tidy cottage, prone in his recliner, cocooned like a newborn in his familiar red-checkered blanket. And the chatter came from Dan, Giddy, Junior, and Samson, huddled around his dining table and talking about him as if he weren't there. Clayton lay still and listened, trying to make sense of it all, trying to remember.

"Can't be outside alone like that," Dan said.

"He's been out alone his entire life," said Giddy.

"Could fall. He's my responsibility now."

"He could fall anywhere, anytime. Here or in a facility."

"We can take turns checking on him," Junior said. "I'm not so busy in the winter. I can make time."

"And during the summer?" Dan asked. "Your hours double. Giddy has the Pet & Play."

Giddy's voice took on urgency. "Summer is months off. Let's worry about summer when it comes."

Samson cut in. "He's OK. Better off than a lot I look after. He has time yet before the next step."

Samson's words stopped them, and they all looked to him, the newcomer.

"I have seen this before," Samson said. "Don't fall apart. Don't make rushed decisions. I'll let you know."

The silence hovered for a moment, no one willing to step into the void. Finally, Dan said, "We'll see it through until summer. Then, who knows?"

Clayton absorbed the word, summer. He drifted back into a dreamscape of his youth and for a while he was a boy again on the marsh in his johnboat setting a line of crab pots and watching a fish hawk on its nest high in the crook of a bald cypress feeding a fish to two chicks. He realized he was almost home now, and was content to remain forever in this place. But the moment passed as he rose to the surface of the conscious world. Outside sounds returned, the scraping of chairs on the wooden floor, a stifled cough from Dan. Clayton opened his eyes and worked the lever on the recliner to partially raise it. "Almost home," he said, groggily.

Dan came from the table and stood in front of Clayton. "Dad, you are home. Look around."

The others followed Dan into the small living area. Fully awake now, Clayton looked from one to the other. "Good to see you," he said. And he meant it.

ACKNOWLEDGMENTS

Thank you, Pamela Kenney Basey and Joey Porcelli for providing review, comment, and encouragement on virtually every story in this collection.

Thanks to Rose Frederick for her insight into an early draft.

Thanks to Steve Almond and Christopher Castellani for offering valuable feedback and for sharing without reservation their encyclopedic knowledge of craft during workshop presentations.

Thanks to publisher, Dr. Ross Tangedal, editor Brett Hill, and the entire staff at Cornerstone Press for a seamless and enjoyable publication process. I appreciate their professionalism, talent, timeliness, and enthusiasm.

Thanks to Lighthouse Writers Workshop for providing the environment that encourages writers to find and develop their voice.

Finally, and always, thanks to Sherri and Will.

GARY SCHANBACHER is the award-winning author of *Crossing Purgatory* (2013), winner of the SPUR Award from the Western Writers of America and the Langum Prize in American Historical Fiction, and *Migration Patterns* (2007), a finalist for the PEN/Hemingway Foundation Award and winner of the Colorado Book Award and the High Plains First Book Award. He lives in the shadows of the Rocky Mountains outside Denver, Colorado.

Printed in the USA
CPSIA information can be obtained
at www.ICGtesting.com
CBHW032010250924
14928CB00003B/61

9 781960 329424